65
D0610426

SPECIAL MESSAGE TO READERS

This book is published under the auspices of

THE ULVERSCROFT FOUNDATION

(registered charity No. 264873 UK)

Established in 1972 to provide funds for research, diagnosis and treatment of eye diseases. Examples of contributions made are: —

A Children's Assessment Unit at Moorfield's Hospital, London.

•

Twin operating theatres at the Western Ophthalmic Hospital, London.

•

A Chair of Ophthalmology at the Royal Australian College of Ophthalmologists.

•

The Ulverscroft Children's Eye Unit at the Great Ormond Street Hospital For Sick Children, London.

You can help further the work of the Foundation by making a donation or leaving a legacy. Every contribution, no matter how small, is received with gratitude. Please write for details to:

THE ULVERSCROFT FOUNDATION,
The Green, Bradgate Road, Anstey,
Leicester LE7 7FU, England.
Telephone: (0116) 236 4325

In Australia write to:
THE ULVERSCROFT FOUNDATION,
c/o The Royal Australian and New Zealand
College of Ophthalmologists,
94-98 Chalmers Street, Surry Hills,
N.S.W. 2010, Australia

IN SEARCH OF TOMORROW

Polly Fletcher's bold decision is to take young brother, Billy, to Australia for a better chance in life. She falls in love with rancher, Jack Peterson, but believing he is not free to marry decides to leave, but Billy runs away unaware he is in danger from a rapidly spreading fire. In the frantic search for Billy, Polly learns the truth about Jack — can she now look forward to a life of sunshine and love . . . ?

JOYCE JOHNSON

IN SEARCH OF TOMORROW

Complete and Unabridged

LINFORD
Leicester

First published in Great Britain in 2010

First Linford Edition
published 2011

British Library CIP Data

Johnson, Joyce, *1931* –
In search of tomorrow. - -
(Linford romance library)
1. Brothers and sisters- -Australia- -Fiction.
2. Ranchers- -Australia- -Fiction.
3. Love stories. 4. Large type books.
I. Title II. Series
823.9'14–dc22

ISBN 978–1–44480–604–5

Published by
F. A. Thorpe (Publishing)
Anstey, Leicestershire

Set by Words & Graphics Ltd.
Anstey, Leicestershire
Printed and bound in Great Britain by
T. J. International Ltd., Padstow, Cornwall

This book is printed on acid-free paper

'He's No Son Of Mine'

Polly Fletcher woke with a start. The bedroom was still dark, just a glimmer of dawn clouded the street outside. Not a good omen for what promised to be such a terrible day, she was reluctant to start it. For a few seconds she lay quietly summing up reserves of strength to face the ordeal.

Her young sister, Annie, was fast asleep, snoring gently beside her. Very carefully Polly folded back the bed covers and stepped out of bed. Raw cold hit her as she hurriedly pulled on the clothes which were neatly folded on the bedside chair.

The small terraced house in the northern town of Castlebridge had been home to her since birth and since her mother's death ten years ago had forced sixteen-year-old Polly to assume her mother's place as chief family carer.

Quietly she crept downstairs to start the day, a day she'd dreaded for weeks, but at least at the end of the day they should know the outcome of young Billy's ordeal. The room downstairs was chilly, only dead ashes in the grate with no trace of last night's warmth.

Shivering, she crumpled old newspapers, laying sticks and coals on top. Her match flared as she lit the paper.

'Go on, catch quickly, give us a good luck omen for the day,' she sat back on her heels and watched the yellow flame slinking round sticks and paper. For a few seconds she was mesmerised by the swift spread of the fire already warming the room. Standing up, she went to the back scullery and filled the copper kettle with water. As she set it on the trivet in the fireplace she heard her father's heavy footsteps on the stairs.

'Polly? It's scarce daylight, why are you up so early?' George Fletcher, thin and stooped, came into the room.

'Dad! Sorry, I didn't mean to wake you. It's just today . . . ' she tailed off as a deep frown furrowed her father's forehead.

He moved towards the fireplace, spreading his hands to the flame. 'That's a champion fire, Polly, warms the heart,' but his face was glum. 'I didn't sleep a wink. Who could with this . . . this thing hanging over us?'

Polly came to stand by her father's chair. 'You've no call to be up so early, so why don't you go back to bed. You don't want to catch cold, you've had a nasty cough and I don't reckon you're better yet. I'll bring you up some tea.'

'No, no it's a sight warmer down here. I couldn't sleep anyhow, all this worry . . . what'll happen, Poll?'

'Hope for the best, Dad, worrying won't help our Billy.'

At the mention of his son's name, George flushed angrily, 'Stupid young fool, times I've warned him, but would he listen? Oh no. I knew how it'd end.' He got up from the chair and a paroxysm of coughing doubled him up, taking his breath away.

Polly ran to the kitchen cupboard, took out a bottle and spoon.

'Here, Dad, swallow this.' She measured out a dose of linctus, pushed her father back into his chair and spooned the medicine into his mouth. 'Calm down now, you know what Dr Wood told you . . . your chest . . . '

'Lungs again,' his voice was wheezy, 'not surprising with all those years down in the pit. You wouldn't keep a dog in those conditions.'

'I know, Dad, but you're retired now so you can take it easy. When it's a bit warmer you can go to your allotment and . . . '

'Warmer? I'm going today — see if my tatties have survived the frost.'

'Surely not today. You can't possibly have forgotten . . . our Billy . . . in court . . . '

'Of course I've not forgotten, though I've tried. God knows, and I'm doing my best to forget him. I warned him until I was blue in the face . . . those . . . those pals,' he spat out the word. 'I told him they were no good and wasn't I right? Wasted my breath . . . '

Polly put a steaming cup of tea on the table, ' . . . and you'll forget him if you've any sense . . . doesn't do our reputation in the neighbourhood any good . . . a jail bird in the family . . . '

'Dad,' Polly raised her voice, 'Billy isn't a . . . jail bird. He says he's done nothing wrong and if he's innocent they'll let him go.'

'Well he would say that, wouldn't he? He's no son of mine. I've no sons any road, not a word from Sam or Fred for . . . well, for how long? Practically a year. Probably dead for all I know.'

'Oh Dad, please. Just keep on believing. Anyway I'm going to court. Billy needs our support.'

'He's forfeited that right, and you can't afford to be off work anyway.'

'Mr Tattersall's given me time off. He's very understanding.'

'He can afford to be — factory owner, sons, grandchildren . . . '

'Right you are, Dad, let's forget it. You go off to your allotment and I'll let you know what happens. Now, I've got some bacon and eggs. Uncle Harry popped in last night with a box of groceries . . . '

'Huh — couldn't eat any of it. I'm not living off his charity.'

'Don't be silly. Dad, he is your brother. He wants to help all he can while he can afford it. Now, I'm going to put bacon and eggs on so you'll soon change your tune. If you don't eat it Annie'll have it. Perhaps after you've had breakfast you'll change your mind and come with me to court. Uncle Harry will be there.'

'Well that's all right then. I'll not be needed.'

Polly shrugged as she lifted down the heavy frying pan, no use arguing once her dad had made his mind up. Since his work had come to an abrupt close, the life had gone out of George Fletcher's world, and with no word from his two eldest sons in Australia he had grown more and more bitter and at odds with the world.

But as the room warmed and the smell of frying bacon reached his nose he began to relax a little. He cocked his head towards the stairs. 'Reckon our Annie's surfaced. Smell of bacon I expect. Will she go with you?'

'She won't. I asked her last night.'

'Shows a bit of common sense then. Can't have both of you without pay, can't live on what pittance I get from the mines,' he spat into the fire, 'compensation for a lifetime wasted underground,' he tailed off gloomily.

'Don't worry, Dad, we'll manage, we always do . . . and if you'd let Uncle Harry help out a bit . . . '

'No! I'll not have that wife of his treating us as a charity case.'

'Come on, Dad,' Polly put a plate on the table, 'you'll feel better when you've had some breakfast.'

'Hello, what's up? Lovely smell, some for me I hope.' Annie Fletcher came to the fire as Polly brought another plate from the kitchen with a mug of tea. 'Oh, lovely — I spy sugar too. Looks like Uncle Harry's been. Hey, you're all dressed up, our Polly. Mr Tattersall promoted you to chief book-keeper?'

'No, I'm going . . . '

'Off to court.' George tucked into his breakfast. 'This is good, Polly. Thanks.'

'Uncle Harry you should thank.'

He grunted, 'Well . . . ' he shrugged and poured out more tea.

'Polly, why are you going to court?' Annie spoke with her mouth full.

'Support Bill of course.'

'Doesn't deserve us,' George said, 'better let the law deal with him. I've done my best. I've no sons any more, my dear Martha gone, bless her, she gave me three boys, but a fat lot of use any of them. Two of them other side of the world, and as for Billy, bringing shame on us.'

'Dad, he's not been proved guilty, he's been in prison for three weeks today and he may be . . . may be freed. I could be bringing him home.'

'Unlikely,' George snorted, 'he's been going downhill these last two years. You've always been too soft on him, Polly. Best he gets locked up, mebbe teach him a lesson.'

'We'll see.' Polly picked up their empty plates and mugs. 'Annie, won't you change your mind and come with me?'

'Goodness, no. Friday's our busiest day and Mr Nightingale relies on me. I could bring some sausages home for tea if there are any left over.'

'That stuff you bring back,' a dark frown had already spread across George Fletcher, 'hope you aren't granting that Nightingale any favours in return.'

'Dad! What a wicked thing to say. That's horrid — and you always eat anything I bring from the shop.'

'Stuff he can't sell then,' George muttered.

Polly banged the table. 'Stop it, the pair of you. I despair, you're always bickering and fighting. I'm going to see what happens to our Billy, he's only eleven years old and our mum would be ashamed of you both. I guarantee if she was alive she'd be in court looking out for Billy.'

There was a heavy silence then Annie sniffed. 'Sorry, our Poll, I don't know how you put up with us. I reckon I can wangle a bit of chicken as well from Mr Nightingale. He'll be sure to give me a good discount anyway, but I do agree with Dad about Billy. He's had lots of warnings about that gang of rogues from Charlotte Street.'

'All the more reason to give him a fresh start,' Polly said.

'Fat chance round here,' George muttered. Agreeing with Annie he said, 'I'm sorry, Poll, I don't know how you put up with me.'

He looked so old, so tired and careworn, Polly gave him a hug. 'Cos you're my dad that's why, and you've not had much luck in life, what with the mine accident and your cough. Mam always used to say, 'never mind, you must be due a change of luck', just you wait and see, she'll be proved right one day.'

'Mmm.' But George patted her hand and looked mollified. 'Take care and wrap up warm then, love.'

'I will. I'm off now, it's a fair old walk to the Court. Hey, if you're going to the allotment see if you've any winter vegetables to go with Annie's possible chicken and sausages.'

'All right, I will.' George looked happier at the prospect of a useful purpose to his day.

'Walk along with me, Annie?'

Her younger sister was combing her fingers through luxuriant blonde curls and admiring herself in the mantel mirror.

'All right, I'll walk part way.' Annie was the beauty of the family: blue eyes, dark blonde hair, a slim figure.

'Just like my poor Martha,' George often said sadly.

The two sisters were a marked contrast. Polly's beauty was less defined: hazel eyes, silky brown hair, and a flawless complexion formed her own good looks. Since Martha Fletcher's death ten years earlier Polly had held the remains of the Fletchers together, and she and Annie were the only breadwinners.

* * *

The sisters huddled into their thick overcoats and tied scarves over their heads. It was bitterly cold, their breaths clouding in the icy air.

'Be glad to reach the shop, at least it's warm in there.'

'Surely not in the shop, meat and all that . . . '

'Ah! I didn't tell you, it's only just been finalised.'

'What is it? You look really excited, Annie.'

'I am. Nightingales are expanding, they've bought next door, you know, the ironmongers. He went bankrupt.'

'That's a shame.'

'Ah well. He's gone to live with his son in America. Florida I think.'

'Lucky him.' Polly thrust her hands deeper into her pockets.

'Anyway, the ex-ironmongers is going to be a café and . . . ' She took a deep breath. 'I'm going to be in charge.'

'Gracious. How wonderful. A café? Fish and chips?'

'Oh no. There's a chip shop on every street corner around here. No, this is to be a proper café. Mrs Nightingale's a champion cook. Proper sit down place, home-made meat pies, sausage and mash. It'll all fit in, you'll see.'

'They must be real pleased with you, Annie, you've only been there twelve months.'

'I can bring more stuff home, a really good discount and — a raise.'

'Annie, that's wonderful.' Impetuously Polly turned to hug her young sister. 'It'll make such a difference. Why didn't you tell us before?'

'Well . . . ' Annie said shortly, 'there is a problem.'

'Ah. I thought it sounded too good to be true.'

'Nay, it might be all right but . . . ' she hesitated, pulled up her scarf close to her face.

'What? What?'

'Well . . . it's . . . young Billy,' she muttered.

'Our Billy? Why, what's the Nightingales' café to do with Billy?'

'Why? Today of course. He's in court. For stealing, stupid boy. I just hope Mr and Mrs Nightingale don't hear about it. You don't suppose it'll be in the newspaper?'

'Almost bound to be. The youngsters round here have been thieving a lot lately.'

Annie stopped in her tracks. 'Oh no. Well that's my prospective job down the drain. Nightingales are great chapel goers so they'd never employ a thief.'

'Annie,' Polly interrupted sharply, 'your brother is not a thief, it's not been proved yet and if he is guilty, which I doubt myself, it's just that he's been in with a bad lot.'

'You're always making excuses for

him. Course he's guilty, police caught the whole lot red-handed.'

'We'll see, but if the Nightingales are true Christians they should be tolerant and forgiving, and even if Billy was guilty it doesn't mean that you're a thief.'

'Ugh. Any road I shan't let on. I just say my prayers and ask God to keep Billy out of the papers.'

'Oh Annie, don't be such a goose.'

'It's all very well for you, you haven't got a . . . ' She stopped, hand to scarf-covered mouth, as if trying to muffle out her words.

'What haven't I got?'

'Er, nothing. Look, here's my turning. I'll see you tonight.'

'No. Tell me what I haven't got?'

'Well, you haven't got . . . got someone who's sweet on you. There, now I've let the cat out of the bag. I'd better get on to Nightingale's. I don't want to be late.'

She turned to go but Polly caught her arm. 'Just a sec, tell me, Annie, who is this person who's sweet on you? It's no crime, you're very pretty, nearly seventeen — what's the problem? Is it our Billy again?'

Annie nodded. 'You see my . . . er . . . it's Donald, Donald Nightingale. He works in the shop with me and he's going to help me manage the new café.'

'Donald Nightingale. The eldest son?'

'Yes.'

'He's a nice boy. A little older than you. Is he serious? You're a bit young to marry.'

'Well, we're not there yet — and don't tell Dad, you know what he's like. I must go, I'll be late. We'll talk tonight when we know about Billy.'

'All right, love, and don't worry. It'll work out, and I'm glad about Donald. I thought you had a spring in your step lately, always desperate to get to work and . . . '

'Don't tease me, Polly, my dreams could so easily turn to dust.'

'Rubbish!' Polly patted her sister's back. 'We'll see nothing does go wrong.'

'I'm sorry, I don't want to think about it yet. Mrs Nightingale's letting me try my hand at the new meat and potato pie recipe today. I'll bring one home, and my wages will increase next week so if our Billy spoils my chances I'll murder him myself.'

There was a weight on Polly's heart as she waved off her sister to the Nightingales' butcher's shop and potential café. 'Please make it all right for Annie,' she sent out a silent prayer on her sister's behalf and turned her face towards the town and the courthouse.

* * *

Ten minutes later Polly was outside the municipal building housing the law courts. A flight of stone steps led to the closed double doors which were guarded by a single policeman as the crowd began to surge forward.

He put out a restraining hand. 'Back please. We're not ready to open yet.'

'Let us in, it's freezing out here.'

'It's beginning to snow . . . '

The policeman pulled out his truncheon as a few bold individuals on the step carried on.

'What's the problem?' Polly asked a woman next to her.

'Don't know, love. Ah, someone's coming out, doors opening now, an official maybe . . . '

'He's my uncle,' Polly couldn't help saying.

'Lucky you then.' The woman disappeared up the steps.

Harry Fletcher, tall, well built, well dressed, had an air of authority Polly had always respected. He was a well known figure in town, a local alderman and sometime magistrate. His path had diverged early from that of his older brother, George. He'd refused to go down the mines but had studied at the local night classes to become a chartered accountant.

To clinch his position in the world he'd married late in life and into money, and was now a managing director of a large department store and clothing company belonging to his wife's father. He'd offered good jobs to both Polly and Annie but their father had refused to allow them to take them, and out of loyalty to their dad both sisters had agreed. Harry Fletcher was also involved in local politics and had ambitions to become a member of parliament.

Now he anxiously scanned the crowd below him and as Polly waved he came to meet her, taking her arm to protect her from the crush.

'Polly, dear, on your own? You shouldn't be. Where's your father? I told him I'd meet you both here.'

'Did you? He never said. He wouldn't come anyway, says he's washed his hands of Billy.'

'Never mind. There's a man keeping a seat near the bench at the front where you'll have a good view of Billy, but you mustn't speak to him.'

'How is he? Have you spoken to him?'

He nodded. 'I wangled a couple of minutes. He's frightened of course, says he hasn't done anything wrong and that he tried to run away from the gang, but they wouldn't let him go. I'm afraid the case against Billy is a strong one and his association with the gang damns him whether he actually took part in the raid or not.'

'Oh goodness. Hopeless is it then?'

'Let's wait and see. Now, I can't sit as a magistrate because Billy is a relative so it wouldn't be proper. I'll see you right after the trial.'

'Will I be able to talk to Billy — afterwards?'

'Probably not if it goes against him.'

'Uncle Harry, what if he has to go to prison . . . ' Polly couldn't keep the sob from her voice.

Harry patted her shoulder. 'Cross that bridge when we come to it. All's not lost yet, I have a few schemes . . . Hush now, they're all in, the magistrate's coming, and there are the boys. See — Billy in the front row.' Harry

Fletcher slipped his niece into a seat near the front at the end of a row and left the room.

Now Polly had a clear view of her young brother and her heart twisted in pity. He was the smallest boy in the group of half a dozen, he was dirty, his clothes were ragged and he looked scared as he tried to hide behind one of the taller boys. She half rose in her seat.

Billy saw her and for a moment his eyes lit up, but as the magistrate called the court to order Billy Fletcher's expression was one of fear and desperation.

A Worrying Time For The Fletchers

In years to come and in better times, Polly could clearly recall the features of Billy's trial; the stern magistrate referring to the notorious Charlotte Street gang, the catalogue of their crimes reeled off by a police officer, some of the gang 'defiantly' outstaring both police officer and magistrate, already hardened criminals set for life in and out of prison.

Now, in the present, Polly's eyes were fixed on young Billy, so small he could hardly see over the dock rail. He looked dirty and frightened, ragged — a street urchin. She could have wept but she forced an encouraging smile when it was Billy's turn to be questioned.

The magistrate looked at him sternly. 'Step forward, Billy Fletcher.'

Polly's heart skipped a beat, Billy hung his head.

'Look at me, boy.' The magistrate was cold.

Billy tried, but Polly knew he was fighting back the tears.

'Sir,' he managed.

'You are the youngest member of this gang of hooligans . . . '

'Please sir, I'm not really . . . '

'Silence, or you will make matters worse for yourself by telling lies. You were caught red-handed in the back rooms of the Station Hotel, identified by the night porter who tells on oath you were carrying two bottles of rum.'

'But . . . sir . . . '

'Quiet. Your age is no excuse and I see from the records you have several times been warned for stealing coal from the coal mine yards.'

'Sir, everyone does that. We only take a bit or two. In the bitter cold . . . '

'That's enough, Billy Fletcher. Your youth is no excuse, you have to learn society will not tolerate such behaviour

— but because you are comparatively young I shall not send you to prison with your fellow thieves but to a house of correction for at least six months. At the end of your sentence you will be birched — six strokes to remind you of your crime. If you appear here again your punishment will be very severe. Take him down, Officer.' He banged the bench with his gavel and pushed aside a pile of papers.

A court officer took hold of Billy's shoulder.

Billy cast an anxious look at Polly.

Near to tears, she smiled encouragement, mouthed, 'See you soon'.

Billy just looked very scared as he was led away.

* * *

In the general movement of preparation for the next trial, Polly slipped out and found room on a bench seat in the main hall where she sat, head in hands, trying to figure a way of seeing her brother, and, even more difficult, how she could help him through his ordeal. 'Polly, what are you doing out here? I was coming to find you in court.'

'Uncle Harry. I'm so glad to see you. Billy . . .'

He nodded. 'I've spoken to one of the lawyers. Six months . . . .'

'It's so unfair.' Polly burst into tears.

'The evidence was strong against him.'

'He never had a chance to explain.'

'At least Billy avoided prison, unlike the rest of the gang.' Harry offered a glimmer of comfort.

'What is a house of correction exactly? Sounds awful.'

'A sight better than prison.'

'Why?'

'In prison he'd spent time with real criminals where he could learn the tricks of an infamous trade and be an apprentice to crime — with men who could easily exploit him.'

'And correction?'

'An attempt to nip crime in the bud. For first offenders like Billy, and youngsters like him, the whole point is to make sure they don't end up in prison.'

'Better than prison then?'

'Better aim, but it's an experiment and very tough. The boys are put to hard work and if they escape then they have even worse punishment.'

'Either way it's horrid for Billy. Can nothing be done?'

'Polly, love, I'm not a miracle worker.'

'You are, you are, look how you helped me, got me to business college, paid it for me, got me the job at Tattersall's, and Annie's at Nightingale's.'

'I was hoping to put you both into Hobson's Department Store, but your dad wasn't happy about that.'

'I know, but Annie and me, we're both fine thanks to you. Annie's happy as a lark and I am too . . . but for Billy of course. You've worked hard all the time I've known you, you've a lovely home, respected in the county and a force in the town. I'm well . . . I'm proud you're my uncle.'

'Hmm . . . well . . . er . . . thanks. I suppose I have worked hard but I've been lucky, too.' He looked at his niece, took off his glasses, polished them, put them back on and paused before he said slowly, 'Well . . . maybe I might just have . . . er . . . a plan, the glimmerings of a solution.'

'What? Uncle Harry, what? Is it Billy?'

'Perhaps . . . '

'Oh, please. Would it help Billy?'

He pulled out his pocket watch. 'Dear, oh dear, it's late, I have a meeting to go to. You're not to worry, Polly. Are you going home or back to work?'

'Work. Mr Tattersall expects me. I've an audit to do.'

He nodded. 'I'll come over to Charlotte Street soon. Dad all right?'

'Chesty. Quite miserable, furious with Billy, refused to do anything for him, off to his allotment even in this weather. Lots of company there, mates from his mining days. He mostly sits in a big shed, puts the world to rights and grumbles a lot.'

Harry laughed. He pulled on expensive leather gloves and glanced again at his watch. 'Oh, one more thing, how's that young man of yours? Jacky Clark, isn't it?'

'Johnny you mean . . . and he's not my young man, just a friend.'

'He thinks highly of you, he told me at chapel last Sunday. Anyway, he's a good steady lad, good prospects too. Training as a schoolmaster.' He gave Polly a shrewd look. 'So no wedding bells yet then?'

'Course not. What an idea, I couldn't leave Dad, and there's Billy too, he'll need me to visit. If you're wanting a wedding in the family maybe you should look to our Annie.'

'Ah, I have heard rumours.'

'Goodness. You've got eyes and ears all over Castlebridge. How do you do it?'

'I keep a watchful eye, but I'll be

missing something important if I don't get a move on.'

They were walking away from the courthouse and facing a bitter wind and a thin wetting drizzle. Polly pulled up her collar.

'On these sort of days I'd swap Castlebridge for a warmer climate any day.'

Harry stopped, puzzled and astonished.

'Really, Polly? I've heard you say lots of times that there's nowhere in the world like Castlebridge.'

'Well, I'm bound to say that, aren't I? This is where I live, my family is here, I just wish it had a better climate. Thanks again for today and I hope to see you soon.' She reached up and kissed his cheek. 'We're jolly lucky to have you in the family, Uncle Harry.' And she was off, striding briskly to her work down the glistening wet street, leaving Harry Fletcher with a strange look on his face.

* * *

Josiah Tattersall was a benevolent Quaker employer who believed that the best workers were the ones best treated. His garment factory on the outskirts of Castlebridge was a model of light and space. Wages were a bit above average and conditions good.

The rain had stopped and a watery smile shone disconsolately on the wet pavements and puddles. To reach the office she shared with Tattersall's chief accountant and Mary, Mr Tattersall's secretary, Polly had to walk through the machinists' floor. She nodded to the women, but was aware of a sudden hush, sympathetic smiles from some, glares of disapproval from others.

Did everyone know of the Fletcher family's shame? Could they possibly already know the outcome of the trial? She hurried towards her office on the second floor.

'Good morning,' Gerald Blake nodded.

'Hello, Polly. Would you like a cup of tea?'

'Oh Mary, I would. It's been a hard morning.'

Mary nodded sympathetically and patted Polly's hand. 'I'll put the kettle on. Oh, Mr Tattersall said for you to go and see him when you got in. He's free now, I'll let him know you're here, then I'll make some tea.'

'Thank you, Mary. I'll just take off my wet things.'

Gerald Blake looked up from his spreadsheets. 'Everything all right, Polly?'

'Yes, thank you, Mr Blake.'

'Good. I'll give you a hand with that audit this afternoon.'

'That'll be good. Thank you.'

Seemed that everyone did know about the morning's events. It'd be all over the local papers no doubt by the end of the week. Nothing to be done except brave it out and stick up for Billy, but she knew that her dad would be furious and fretting, and as for Annie . . .

'Go in, Polly,' Mary urged, 'Mr Tattersall's expecting you.'

'Nothing wrong?'

'Oh no, I shouldn't think so. Just a chat, kettle's on, I expect you could do with a cup of tea afterwards.' She turned back to her typewriter and gave Polly a sympathetic smile.

'Come in, come in.' Josiah Tattersall stood up and ushered Polly to a chair. He peered at her closely. 'Are you all right? Bit of an ordeal this morning.'

'Well, yes, but how does everyone seem to know about it?'

'Local grapevine I suppose, and your uncle is a very well-known figure in town. He has spoken to me this morning, that's how I know the outcome of the trial. We belong to the same lodge and . . . '

'Oh — of course.'

'Your brother, Billy — a great worry for you.'

Polly felt tears rising, sternly pushed them down. 'I still believe Billy is innocent, he's just in with the wrong gang of boys.'

'Well, I suppose . . . ' But obviously

Mr Tattersall was on the side of the sceptics.

'Are you going to sack me, Mr Tattersall?'

'Sack you? Why ever should I do that? Best bookkeeper I've had in years.'

Polly gave a sigh of relief. 'So you don't mind . . . about our Billy?'

'Of course I mind, he's been very foolish, but maybe a spell in Correction will make him see sense. It's not your fault, I know you're doing everything you can for your family. You most certainly don't deserve the sack, Polly Fletcher.'

'Thank you, Mr Tattersall. You're very kind.'

'Not kind, it's Christian charity, Polly. I just hope your Billy comes through his ordeal — a sinner can always repent. I believe your uncle has a plan.'

'He hints at something. Do you know anything about it?'

'No, no, of course not, but I know he wants to do his best for your family.

He's quite a power in the town and hoping to stand for parliament in the future maybe. I'm glad the trial's over anyway, at least Billy can't get into any more mischief for a while.'

With that comforting thought Polly returned to her office and started work, glad to have something absorbing to keep her mind occupied.

* * *

Meanwhile, Harry Fletcher, in his well-appointed office on the top floor of Hobson's Department Store was making telephone calls and sending telegrams both locally and internationally. After an hour or so he sat back in his chair and called for a pot of coffee.

'Busy morning, sir.' His secretary put the tray on his desk.

'Quite, Alice. I see the store's gratifyingly busy today.'

'Sale time, always is. There are lots of bargains and good staff discounts.'

'Good, good, that's what I like to

hear. Now, give me ten minutes then, if you would, put a call through to my wife.'

As he drank his coffee Harry turned to store business, a business which was nominally owned by his wife, Victoria. Her late father had built up Hobson's from a small market stall to one of the county's leading department stores with several branches throughout the north of England.

When Frank Hobson died the stores passed to his only daughter, Victoria Hobson. Unfortunately Victoria had no interest in the business apart from spending the profits on lunch parties, clothes, and trips to France. With no strong hand at the helm the stores began to flounder and even Victoria could see financial ruin ahead. She began to panic, took bad advice and plunged towards bankruptcy.

Frank Hobson had always provided a fine Christmas party for his staff and, at what Victoria believed would be the last affair of these, a Christmas angel came to the rescue in the shape of Harry Fletcher, chief buyer for Hobson's stores. Harry, in his late thirties, was a handsome, confident man, unmarried, with a good business head, and dedicated to the future of Hobson's Department Stores. He came on to the scene just in time. He and Victoria were married within a year, Victoria delighted for Harry to take full charge of the business.

Under Harry's management the business turned around into profit, and Victoria produced a son. It was a difficult birth which she declared would be the last and only one by Victoria. She had done her duty providing a son and heir and she could devote her time and energy to hunt balls and charity events where she could organise support for her growing ambition to be the wife of an M.P. — and then take Westminster by storm!

She had little patience with the lowly part of the Fletcher family in Charlotte Street, avoiding social contact if at all possible and shutting her ears to current rumours about the family's troubles.

Harry pushed aside his business papers, poured a second cup of coffee and reached for the telephone. 'Alice, could you get my wife on the phone now?'

'Certainly, Mr Fletcher.'

'Harry? What is it? I'm due at Vincent's. I'm already late.'

'Is Wilf all right?'

'Wilfred? Yes, yes, of course. Nanny's taking him to the park.'

'What? Surely not in this weather. He'll catch a chill and . . . '

'Don't be silly and don't fuss, the boy needs fresh air. Is that what you wanted me for?'

'No. I want us to visit George, my brother.'

'I know who George is,' she said impatiently. 'Why do I need to go?'

'Because . . .' Harry closed his eyes — he loved his wife, admired her various skills, and was ever conscious he owed her his wealthy and comfortable life style — and, of course, she had given him Wilfred, his beloved son. But it was at a cost. Victoria was a snob and he knew without her outright saying so that she was ashamed of his Charlotte Street family and rather wished they lived much farther away. As it was, she tried hard to avoid social contact with them.

' . . . because I want you to come with me to see George and his family.' There was silence. 'Victoria?'

'All right. When?'

'Soon as possible. Tonight? Tomorrow?'

'I'm really busy, Harry. There's a ball . . . can't you go on your own? I'll come another time.'

'No. Now is when they need our support, Victoria, and George is always asking about you. He isn't at all well and . . . '

'I know, I'm sorry for him but that wretched boy, Billy . . . I try to shut him out of my mind.'

'Billy was sentenced in court today . . . '

'I don't want to know,' she interrupted sharply.

'He's our nephew, Victoria.'

'More's the pity. He's nothing to do with me.'

'Please, Victoria. What if it was our Wilfred?'

'Don't be preposterous. There's no comparison.'

'The difference is that our boy will have a better start than Billy had. I insist you come with me.'

A deep sigh, then, 'Oh, very well. Maybe next Thursday afternoon.'

'As you know I am at work in the daytime and so are Polly and Annie. I need them to be there, as well as George.'

'Why?'

'I've a plan. May help them but it's,' he paused, searching for the right words, 'quite drastic. I need your opinion — whether it's the right thing to do.'

'What sort of plan?'

'I'll tell you when I've worked out some more details. I need your opinion, I respect your common sense, Victoria. It may be quite out of the question.'

'You can't get round me with flattery, but I suppose I must come with you . . . but promise we won't stay long.' Harry sensed her shudder. 'I do find that little . . . house so depressing. Can't you really go on your own?'

'No, I can't. Victoria, extend charity work to your own family for once. I absolutely insist you come and we will take Wilfred too. It's time he got to know his relatives.' He put the phone down quickly, cutting off more of his wife's potential protests.

A Shocking Plan Is Offered

'Annie, is the table set? Have you checked the pies in the oven? Visitors'll be here soon,' Polly called out from the seldom used front parlour. 'Come on,' she muttered, holding a newspaper across the fireplace to encourage the fire to draw and warm up the chilly room.

At the door Annie coughed. 'Table set, pies fine. I told you not to light that dratted thing, we'll be suffocated by all that smoke. Most likely chimney's blocked, can't remember when we last used this room.' She sighed. Mam's pride and joy was reserved for special occasions, mainly funerals. She held a handkerchief to her mouth as she watched her sister struggle with the sulky coals. 'Best leave it, it's much warmer in the kitchen — roaring fire in the range.'

'Annie, we can't all sit in there, not enough chairs for a start.'

'We've a couple of bedroom chairs, I'll easily bring them down. Heavens, Polly, we're not expecting royalty to pay us a call — it's family, and, did I mention, Donald might drop in later. He wants to meet our posh relatives.'

'Oh Annie, not tonight. You must put him off.'

'Too late, he's coming straight from the shop. Don't you want to meet him?'

'Course I do, you daft thing, but what with Uncle Harry and Aunt Victoria . . . she's only been here a couple of times, and baby Wilfred's never been. Donald's not coming for supper, is he?'

'Shouldn't think so, he's working every hour possible to get the café started.'

'Oh well, we'll manage. Maybe the more the merrier. Fire's catching nicely, the room'll soon warm up.' Polly set a fireguard around the grate and glanced at the mantel clock. 'Annie, move yourself, they'll be here in five minutes. Is Dad tidy?'

'Yes, and he's in his Sunday best suit. He doesn't look too comfortable in it. Last wore it at Tommy Lunn's funeral, smells of mothballs.' She giggled, 'Make her ladyship get her lace hanky out, I bet.'

Polly gave her a stern look. 'Now then, you just behave yourself, best manners. Uncle Harry's very good to us and I won't have him upset.'

'I won't upset him, but Queen Victoria's a different matter. Bet he had to bribe her to set foot in Charlotte Street.'

'Hush, there's the car. It'll be them. Let them in.'

She ran to the front door, Annie following more slowly, twisting blonde strands of hair round her fingers. 'Uncle Harry, Aunt Victoria, come in, come in. Annie, help carry those parcels. Whatever have you brought, Uncle?'

'Oh, nothing much, some ale, bottle or two of wine . . .'

'Wine?' Annie's eyes widened. 'Let me take it.' She proffered her cheek to her uncle, then to Victoria who pecked the air and smiled.

'Why, Annie, what a pretty girl you are.'

'Ah, thank you. That's because you haven't seen me for . . . what, a couple of years at least, Aunt Victoria.'

'Really? How remiss of me. I must put that right in future . . . er, George, how are you?'

'I'm fine now,' George's voice seemed stronger, 'good to see you, Harry, Victoria and young Wilfred. He's a handsome little chap.' He leaned over and held out a tentative hand to his nephew.

Wilfred grasped it with a chuckle.

'See he's taken to you straight off,' Harry said.

'Humph — there's fat chance of getting to know the lad, hardly seen him but a couple of times . . . '

'Tea's ready.' Polly said hastily, 'draw up to the table. Bit of a squash, can you manage Wilfred, Auntie? I tried to borrow a high chair.' She and Annie bustled in and out of the kitchen with hot savoury dishes. 'I mashed up some vegetables for Wilfred, vegetables and gravy, is that right, Auntie?'

'Well . . . er . . . I . . .'

'I've bought him a china dish. Look, rabbits, birds on the edges.'

'Well . . . er . . . I suppose. Mealtimes are Nanny's job usually.' Victoria was unused to supervising her son's meal-times.

Steaming hot savoury pies, dishes of chips, followed by Polly's homemade fruitcake, softened the atmosphere and even Victoria's chilly demeanour thawed under the influence of a glass of Harry's wine.

'A grand meal, girls,' Harry comm-ented as fruitcake and cheese were brought out.

Harry helped himself to a large slice of cake just as the front door bell rang.

Annie leapt up to her feet. 'That'll be Donald, he said he'd pop by, say hello to everyone.'

'Donald?' Victoria looked alarmed, the small room was already over-crowded. It was hot and stuffy and for Wilfred the novelty of his relatives had worn off. He began to grizzle.

'Ah, he's tired. We'd better get him home, Harry.'

'Nay, you've only just come.' George, in spite of himself, was enjoying the unaccustomed company. 'If you nurse the babby, Victoria, you can stay a bit longer.'

'But . . . '

'Do as George says please, Victoria,' Harry said, 'I need to talk seriously to George and Polly and Annie.'

'Oh, surely you can do that another time. Nanny . . . '

'Has a night off, I checked, and I want you here, Victoria. What I have to say could concern you as well. Ah . . . what's this, Annie, I didn't expect you'd have any other company.'

'Uncle Harry, this is Donald Nightingale. Um . . . the baker's where I work. His dad's shop and café. He wants to meet you.'

A tall dark-haired young man stepped forward, nodded to the assembled company and shook, first Harry's hand, then George's.

'Pleased to meet you both, sir. Annie's told me about you. I believe you are in my father's Lodge.'

'I am. He has a fine family business. Expanding so I hear.'

'Yes. We have lots of plans and I hope to include Annie in those plans.' He put his hand on Annie's shoulder. 'That's why I wanted to meet her family.'

'I'm Annie's father,' George frowned, 'and if you've any intentions towards our Annie I am the person for you to address, young man — and this is hardly the occasion — as you can see . . . '

'Dad!' Annie retorted sharply, 'I wanted Donald to meet everyone.'

'I understand that,' Harry said, 'but I

have something important to discuss here. A family matter.'

'Of course. I'll leave, I didn't intend to stay for long.'

Victoria stood up, a sleepy Wilfred hoisted on her shoulder. 'This child should be in his bed. He's too heavy for me to hold.'

Harry frowned. 'His Moses basket is in the car and Wilfred could sleep in that. It won't hurt for once.'

'Can I fetch it?' Donald asked. 'Then I'll leave.'

'That would be kind, and Polly — you said there's a fire in the other room. Perhaps we'd be more comfortable in there.'

'A fire,' George exploded, 'what's that for?'

'Well it's done now, there's more room there and a nice corner for Wilfred's basket.'

'What's going on, and who was that young man who was here a minute ago?' George grasped his stick and tried to stand up.

'Donald was here to meet the family, I just told you, Dad,' Annie said in exasperation. 'We're . . . we are courting, that's why he was here.'

'Courting? First I've heard. You . . . you haven't got to get wed have you?'

'Dad!' Polly admonished as Annie spoke.

'We . . . we want to get engaged, that's why he was here tonight.'

'Could have chosen a more private moment,' George snapped.

'Here we are.' Donald put the wicker basket on the floor. 'Let me.' He carefully took the baby from Victoria and placed him carefully in the basket, covered him up and turned the basket away from the light. 'Flat out, fast asleep.' Seeing Victoria's startled expression he laughed, 'Lots of practice you see, younger sisters. Big family, the Nightingales.' He took Annie's hand. 'See you tomorrow at the shop. Thank you, Mr Fletcher, perhaps I may call again at a more convenient time to you.'

George grunted, 'Don't mind me, no one else does.'

'Don't be so grumpy, Dad, you want me to be happy, don't you? I'll see Donald out.'

As they left the room Polly picked up the brown teapot. 'Er, more tea — or shall we move into the parlour?'

'Good idea.' Harry stooped to pick up the Moses basket. 'Or shall I leave him here and we can pop in and keep an eye on him? He's fast asleep right now.'

Victoria shrugged. 'Please yourself, as long as we don't stay too long. Nanny hates Wilfred's routine to be disrupted.'

'Well she'll have to get used to it then, won't she? I think we'd best find him a little corner in the parlour. You can keep an eye on him, Victoria.'

It was warm and cosy in the little sitting room. Polly brought Harry's wine and whisky and settled George nearest the fire, a glass of whisky for him on the side table. Annie, somewhat flushed, joined them and accepted a glass of wine from Harry who had poured himself another whisky, seemingly reluctant to start proceedings.

'This room — reminds me so much of dear Martha,' he said nostalgically, 'her pride and joy, wasn't it, George?'

'I thought you had something to tell us,' George replied grumpily, 'best get on with it.' He took a sip of whisky and relaxed back in his chair.

'Is it anything to do with our Billy?' Polly asked eagerly.

'Oh no, please.' Annie looked at her aunt who shrugged her shoulders with a 'nothing to do with me' expression, and got up to check on the baby in the basket, turning her back on her husband.

'Come back and sit down, Victoria,' Harry said very sharply, 'I want everyone's full attention.'

Unaccustomed to a sharp tone from her husband Victoria sat down.

'I'm sorry that Donald had to leave, Annie. He seems a very nice young man, from a good family. I hope things go well, but what I have to say is very private and confidential. I . . . we . . . Billy could be in trouble if I'm not careful.' Now he had their full attention, the room was still, the only sound being Wilfred's tiny baby snore from the basket.

'Well, Harry?' Victoria broke the silence after a covert glance at her fob watch. 'Are you going to keep us all in suspense much longer? We should be leaving soon.'

'All right.' Harry pulled out some papers from a leather case. 'These papers,' he held them up, 'could secure Billy's release from the correction house.'

'Uncle Harry!'

'What? How?'

'Don't mock us,' George said reproachfully.

'As if I would. I'm very serious, George, and I tell you I've been to a great deal of trouble to . . . um . . . fix this — expense, string-pulling, calling in of favours . . . '

'All right, I'm sorry, but let's hear it . . . what you've got to say.' George leaned forward and faced his brother. 'How could you do this, you're not a miracle worker. Billy's got what he deserves anyway.'

'I'll explain then. You know . . . we . . . town council, police, magistrates, and ordinary citizens . . . just read your local paper — there's been a real rise in juvenile crime — prison, correction houses, reform schools, but none of them seem to be working . . .

'That's the whole point. Billy will be tempted back into crime, once he's out it'll be prison next, too. He'll have had his chance. So, myself and a group of a few concerned fellow citizens have hit on an idea, a scheme which would fit our Billy to a T, and suit us all too.'

'All of us?' Victoria raised her eyebrows.

'Let me explain,' Harry put in quickly, 'what Billy wants . . . needs, is a fresh start, to get away from here and the bad influences — a need to get right away.'

'Away?' Polly and Annie spoke in unison.

'Where to?' Polly added, her eyes troubled.

'Well, in previous years . . . ' Harry hesitated, 'a fresh start for young offenders was transportation to the colonies, certain . . . '

'Convicts?' Victoria breathed in horror. 'A convict in the family . . . '

'Do be quiet, Victoria, and let me explain. Billy is not quite a convict — yet, and I and one or two influential men have proposed a scheme to the police and magistrates. Our colonies are desperate for young people to live and work — in Australia for example, rich in gold and vast lands for farming.'

'Australia?'

'You can't mean our Billy?'

'It's ridiculous.'

'It could have its advantages . . . ' Victoria said slowly, spotting a lopping off of the embarrassing Charlotte Street family branch.

Harry ignored her. 'Previously boys as young as Billy were transported for quite minor crimes without any guarantee of support when they got there, or little idea of what would happen to them when they finally reached their destination. I thought Billy and all his family could benefit from such a scheme; a new life, new country. Of course, Billy would be under supervision . . .'

'Whose supervision?' Polly was white-faced. 'He's only eleven years old. We can't let him go across the world on his own . . .'

'Not on his own, of course not. You haven't been listening at all. Obviously that's not the plan, and there's still a lot to decide, it's early days. It would be a pilot scheme, no publicity or we'd have every criminal in prison wanting this sort of opportunity.'

'But it's ridiculous,' Polly cried, 'our Billy will be out of the correction house in six months. We can look after him, make sure he doesn't . . .'

'Doesn't what, Polly? He'll revert to crime, most do, and Billy's shown he's easily led; believe me, I know what I'm talking about.'

'It's a good scheme,' Victoria chipped in.

'Would you send Wilfred away like that?' Polly asked sharply.

'Well of course not, there's no comparison . . . '

Harry tapped the table. 'Stop. Let's put this in perspective. We've no intention of sending Billy away on his own, that's crazy, but you'd all go with him, passages paid, jobs for Polly and Annie. I have a lot of business interests in Australia, valuable contacts.'

Victoria gasped, 'What sort of . . . ? I didn't know . . . '

'Well you've never really been interested in my business life, my dear. I don't want to bore you, but I have other irons in the fire apart from Hobson's.'

'You really think you can get rid of us by sending us to Australia?' George's face was dangerously flushed.

'I'm not getting rid of you. It's a way out for Billy, and you're not committed to stay there forever if you don't like it. Just time enough for Billy to get back on track, and just think, George, lots of sunshine, no more coughs and colds.'

'Nonsense, my lungs are already damaged and beyond repair. I'm not budging. Billy Fletcher's made his bed, he can lie in it.'

'Dad!' Polly shook her head.

Annie shook back her curls. 'Well, I'm not going to Australia, I'm very happy here — with the Nightingales.'

'I'm sorry, Annie,' Harry said, 'I'd no idea you were thinking of getting wed. You'll have to talk to Donald.'

'No need thank you, Uncle Harry. Castlebridge'll do for me — and what about Johnny Clark, Polly, what'll he have to say about it?'

'I've told you, we're just friends, he doesn't matter, it's Billy I'm concerned about. There's no understanding between Johnny and me, we're just friends.'

The silence was strained until baby

Wilfred stirred in his sleep and began to whimper.

'See what you've done, Harry Fletcher?' Victoria stood up. 'I told you, Wilfred's routine is broken. It seems your great idea isn't all that popular. Billy Fletcher will just have to take his medicine, and that's that.'

Harry put his papers back in his case and shook his head sadly.

'Billy has no chance, I've seen it over and over. I've done my best but if you won't even consider it . . . come along then, Victoria. I'll keep an eye out for Billy in the correction house. Lovely supper, good to see you.'

'Wait, Uncle Harry.' Polly stopped him putting his papers away. 'Tell me more about your plan. Is it possible for me to go with Billy — just me?'

Journey To A New World

Stunned silence at the notion Polly and Billy might travel to the other end of the world, possibly for the duration.

Victoria broke the silence. 'Is it possible, Harry? Billy and Polly, on their own?'

Annie interrupted swiftly. 'Course she can't go, leave Castlebridge? Impossible.'

'But it is possible, Uncle Harry?' Polly spoke directly to her uncle whose face registered amazement, relief and, strangely, apprehension.

'My dear, do you know what you're saying?'

'Of course I do. You said it yourself. Billy needs a fresh start and he has changed in prison. On my last visit to him he wasn't my little brother, he hardly spoke to me, he was . . . well, he was surly and scared. I hated leaving him and I've fretted over him all these weeks. If there's a glimmer of hope I'm prepared to do anything, go anywhere.'

'Who'd look after me?' George Fletcher burst out. 'I can't do without our Polly.' His voice trembled, 'Don't leave me, lass.'

Polly knelt by his chair. 'Dad, I have to if it's possible, and Annie will be here, and your brother, and Aunt Victoria.'

'It'll not be the same. I forbid you to go.'

'I don't think you can, Dad, I'm twenty-one years old, responsible for my own future and, whatever happens, I'd come back and visit you, and maybe, if Billy and I like it in Australia it'd do you good to come out to a warmer climate.'

'It's not right,' George muttered, 'and it's all that boy's fault.' He tried to get up, started coughing and collapsed back into his chair.

'And what about me,' wailed Annie, 'I'm not stopping work to look after

Dad. There's Donald, too — we want to get married.'

'You can't,' George spluttered, 'you're only fifteen . . . '

'I'm sixteen, Dad, for goodness sake, seventeen next month. You and Mam married when she was sixteen.'

'That's not the point, girl, I need someone here to look after me. You must give up your job and your fancy man to . . . '

'Dad!' from both daughters.

'You see,' Annie was almost sobbing. 'Polly, I can't manage him, you mustn't leave us . . . '

A sudden wail from the cot added to the commotion and alerted Victoria to her maternal responsibilities. She picked Wilfred up and rocked him gently in her arms.

'Harry,' she said softly, 'is it really possible for Polly to go out with Billy, just the two of them?'

'Well, my plan was for them to emigrate as a family, for Billy's sake that's the obvious way.' He turned to

Polly, 'My dear, it would be terribly hard for you, on your own. Billy, for a start would be a big responsibility and there's no knowing . . . '

'But is it possible?' Polly persisted, 'just tell me that.'

Harry thought for a few moments staring at the papers on the table, 'Of course, anything's possible. As I said I've got many contacts in Western Australia, mining interests in Kalgoolie, contacts in Fremantle but . . . '

'Can you afford to pay for both of us?'

'Well, of course. I expected to pay for the whole family. Maybe there could be government assistance and I thought maybe . . . maybe you could make enquiries about Sam and Fred when you were out there.'

'I know you've made lots of enquiries, Uncle Harry,' Polly said, 'but maybe if I was actually there . . . '

'Mebbe. Mebbe. Could be!' George exclaimed bitterly. 'Both sons probably dead, Annie wedded, you going off, and as for that lad, Billy,' he almost spat out the word, 'a jailbird, a convict, no son of mine. I'm glad my Martha died before she saw it . . . '

'Oh Dad,' Polly put a hand on his shoulder, 'don't speak so. If you're so strongly against it we'll just wait for Billy to come home from the correction house and keep a strict eye on him, but . . . Dad, I have to tell you now, I promised Mam when she was dying just after our Billy was born, she made me promise to look after Billy.'

'Only natural she would,' George muttered, 'you're the eldest.'

'I was only twelve then, Dad, but I did promise. Mam made me swear on the bible and also to keep that promise secret, which I have done until now. Mam said over and over 'Billy's special, keep him safe for me, Polly'.' Her voice broke, recalling that sad moment nine years earlier. 'I've tried to keep that promise,' she said quietly, 'but I've failed both Mam and Billy, and if there's the opportunity I want to put it right. So, please, Uncle Harry, will you help me?'

Harry looked across to his scowling brother. George?' He asked quietly.

'Aye, go ahead, do what you want, nowt I say will change anything. I'm done for any road.'

'Oh come on, George, pull yourself together,' Victoria spoke sharply as she jiggled Wilfred up and down. 'Good for you, Polly, best thing you could do, new horizons, and I tell you what, I'll personally guarantee to keep an eye on your dad, and Annie, too, if you want. As for coping, George, it'll do you good, give you something to think about for a change. I'll send some of my . . . um . . . our house staff to keep an eye on you.

'So you see, Harry, you have no alternative but to set up this Australia venture. After all, if you really hate it, Polly, you can always come home, we'll all still be here. Now, do come along, Harry, this baby needs his cot.' Victoria Fletcher had a social conscience, but she'd had enough of Harry's family for one night.

* * *

Billy Fletcher was to serve another four weeks of his sentence before he was taken by a policeman to the railway station to meet up with Polly and the family. It was a strange reunion, a curious little party.

George Fletcher, muffled up to the eyes, barely looked at his young son. 'Behave yourself,' he growled, then forced out, 'do as your sister tells you,' before he turned away to stare moodily up the railway track.

Polly hugged Billy but he stiffened and pulled away, looking warily around as though the police officer would grasp him suddenly to force him back to prison.

Harry was going with Polly and Billy to York station where they would see them on to The Flying Scotsman to London.

'Here's the train.' Annie, half tearful, hugged her sister. 'Polly, Polly, don't go.'

'I must, and you'll manage. I'll write the minute we get to Australia. Look after Dad.'

'I'll try. I really will.'

'Dad,' Polly hugged him, 'you look after our Annie too.'

George Fletcher managed a weak smile.

'Come on, Polly,' Harry was already on the train as she and Billy climbed aboard.

Doors slammed, the guard blew his whistle, and Polly leaned out of the window to wave goodbye to her family, her heart anxious, tears threatening. Billy, pale-faced, stayed huddled in a corner, simply staring out of the window as the train slid out of the station.

'Come on, Billy, next to me,' Polly put her arms round him

He held away at first, then slowly relaxed against her.

Harry smiled encouragingly. 'There, worst is over, you're on your way. Polly, you've got all your papers? Passports, tickets, letters of introduction. You'll be met at Fremantle — Mr Dick Potter.'

'Yes, Uncle, we've been through it lots of times. I know what I've got to do — off by heart.'

'Good girl. Let's enjoy the trip then, we'll have time for lunch in York before the London train. It's a great adventure, Polly love.'

'It's good of you to come to York with us, Uncle Harry.'

'Don't tell anyone, but I'm really coming to have a look at The Flying Scotsman. I wish I could travel to London with you.'

'We'll be fine, Uncle.'

'Are we going all the way to Australia on this train?' Billy asked.

'Heavens no, by sea from London docks.'

'Will I be in the prison there?'

'Course not, you old silly. Uncle Harry's booked us a nice little cabin and there'll be lots to do and see.'

In no time it seemed the train drew into York station. Harry looked at his watch. 'Oh dear, we're a little late, hardly time for lunch I'm afraid, but there'll be a buffet on The Flying Scotsman. Look, see over there waiting. Isn't it a magnificent sight?'

Polly and Billy were ready to board the train, a quick hug from Harry, final instructions, repeat warnings, doors slammed, the guard blew his whistle, waved his flag and they were off.

* * *

'How much longer?' Billy yawned several hours later.

'A few hours yet. Are you still hungry, we didn't have much time for lunch? I've got some bread and cheese.' Polly stood up to reach a bag in the luggage rack. 'Now, where did I . . . ' she rummaged among the bags, 'Here . . . Billy?' She turned round, 'Billy? Where . . . ?' but the boy had gone. 'Billy . . . ' she was now frantic.

'He's gone,' a woman said.

'Oh no. Which way?'

The woman pointed up the train. 'I think,' she whispered to Polly, you know, he needed to . . . '

'Oh goodness.'

'You'll catch up with him, can't be gone far.'

'Oh heavens, why didn't he say?'

'Off you go after him, I'll keep an eye on your baggage . . . '

'Thanks.' Polly, in the corridor, ran towards the front of the train looking for any sign of her brother. As she went from one carriage to another she bumped into a man carrying a small case.

'Hey, sorry. Er . . . are you all right?' A tall man, dark hair, very blue eyes, looked at her quizzically, 'Not a fire, is there?'

'Worse,' she almost sobbed, 'my little brother . . . I can't find him.'

'Youngster, about eleven or twelve, blond . . . '

'Yes, yes, have you seen him?'

'Surely . . . he's in there.' The man pointed to the toilet.

'Oh, thank heavens. Please, do you mind . . . could you get him out of there?'

'I can try.' He rattled the door. 'Locked, he'll be out in a minute.'

'I . . . I don't know. Billy, Billy,' she called but there was no sound. Billy, oh Billy, it's only Polly. Come out, please.'

A frightened cry from inside, 'I can't, the lock won't work.'

'Let me,' the man put his shoulder to the door and pushed. It gave way at once. 'See, easy, not properly locked.' He smiled. 'Must have got it stuck somehow. Come out, Billy, your sister's here.' The man had a slight accent which Polly couldn't place.

'Billy,' she scolded, 'why didn't you ask me? I was just getting some food. Thank you,' she said to the man.

He put out his hand. 'Pleased to help. Jack Peterson. You going to London?'

'Yes. Thank you, we'd best get back

to our seats. Thank you again, Mr Peterson.'

'I'm just going to the buffet car, would you and Billy . . . ?'

'Oh, thank you but no, we're . . . we're . . . I've got some water and bread.'

'Oh well, perhaps later.' He ruffled Billy's hair. 'You look after your sister, young man, and don't give her such a fright again. Sure you won't join me?'

'Oh no, thanks. Come on, Billy.' But as she pulled Billy along the corridor she began to think it would have been nice to have gone along with the handsome stranger. After all, this was to be a great adventure, wasn't it? 'Don't do that again, Billy love, all you had to do was ask me.'

'I was scared,' he snuffed.

'Whatever of? Of me!'

'No, but . . . but back in that place . . . the other boys . . . ?'

'Bullied you? Tell me, Billy.'

'No. No, it's all right now, now I'm with you, Polly — and we're going a long way from those boys now, aren't we?'

'We most certainly are, and you and I, well, we can do anything. It'll be a grand new life for us in Australia.'

* * *

Polly and Billy's life began the moment they walked up the gangplank of S.S. *Orient*, destination Fremantle, Western Australia. The steamship's two large funnels were already belching back smoke when Polly finally found their cabin which was small but comfortable, larger than the room she'd shared with Annie back in Castlebridge. Still clutching her precious bag she sat on the bottom bunk.

'Well, Billy, feeling better now? This is our home for about forty days now. We'll unpack then explore.'

Still white-faced and uncertain, Billy nodded.

Polly put her arms around him. 'Don't worry now, you're safe here, no-one's going to bully you on this ship. Just stay close to me and, Billy love, let's enjoy this.'

The S.S. *Orient* was to sail from London to Fremantle via the Suez Canal, Egypt and India. In the 1900s the new steam ships provided many amenities and improved facilities for emigrants. There was more space for recreation, promenade decks, games areas. To Polly and Billy it was a new and wonderful world, a far cry from the cold back streets of Northern England. Sea air and sunshine put a healthy gloss to their sun-starved skins and gradually they made friends with other emigrants.

Billy joined in games of quoits, ping pong or shuffleboard. He gradually lost his hunched-up wary posture. Polly swore he grew at least three inches during the voyage.

'How long will we be on the ship?' he frequently asked.

'About forty days altogether before we reach Fremantle. Will you be glad?'

‘No. I like it here, Polly, can’t we just stay forever?’

Polly laughed. ‘You’d soon get bored, and we haven’t met a real storm yet. We’ve been lucky.’

One day, towards the end of the long voyage, Billy came running to his sister who was sunning herself on the deck. ‘Polly, we just had a peep in first class, it’s magic.’

‘Billy, that is not allowed under any circumstances. You’d be punished if they found you.’

‘Aw, we only had a peep. It’s a room with a grand piano! And gold ornaments! Palm trees, and I saw that man in there.’

‘Billy, that’s very naughty and you must never do it again. We are very happy here, no need to go poking your nose in where you’re forbidden to go. Promise . . . ’

‘But he smiled at me, he didn’t care we shouldn’t be there. He was with a lovely looking lady. She didn’t see us.’

‘What man?’

'The man on the train, when I was locked in . . . '

'Oh, that one. Well, it's a good job he didn't report you.'

'He wouldn't do that, he saw me and winked.'

* * *

Eventually the 'holiday' had to end as the west coast of Australia loomed on the horizon and the huge ship slowly docked in Fremantle Harbour to a fanfare of music greeting the steamship's safe arrival. All passengers' class divisions were temporarily waived, and they lined the rails to scan the crowd, some waving wildly, convinced they'd spotted waiting friends and relatives.

Polly clutched her bag with all her introduction papers, she was to be met by a friend of Uncle Harry's, Dick Potter. The name was stamped on her brain. He wouldn't be amongst the crowd on the dockside. Harry had told her they would have to go through the procedures of the immigration authorities which might take some time. She was not to worry, if by any remote chance Dick Potter didn't turn up, another of Harry's business contacts would be there.

She stared at the crowds, apprehension stirred in her stomach, she didn't want to leave the safety of the ship. She felt a hand on her shoulder and spun round.

'Ah, so I didn't dream it?' a tall man, dark hair, blue eyes, smiled down at her, his eyes warm and friendly. 'What a coincidence. I recognised your brother.'

'Oh, yes. You're the man on the train.' She blushed at the recollection, 'I'm sorry, Billy had no business to be there in first class.'

'No problem. He was only on the fringe, no harm done. Where are you going?' He spoke with a slight Australian accent which she hadn't placed on the train in England. 'Have you friends here?' he asked.

'Er . . . no . . . my uncle has . . . er . . . friends, contacts in Fremantle.'

'Oh, so you're taken care of.' He looked puzzled. 'Are you staying here or just visiting — a holiday perhaps?'

Polly had to laugh. They'd had a holiday on the ship and what lay ahead she had no idea, but it certainly wouldn't be a holiday.

The stranger was looking at her oddly. 'You're sure you'll be all right? If I can help . . . '

'No, no, I . . . we'll be fine. Thank you.'

At that moment a woman grasped his arm from behind, 'Jack, do come on. Ellie is waiting for us, I've spotted her in the crowd.'

'All right, Ma, I'm coming. Is Julie ready to embark?' but he still lingered, watching Polly, until the older woman literally pulled him away to be swallowed up in the masses lining up to go down the gangplank, some including Polly and Billy to take their first steps in the unknown new continent.

Polly was sorry the stranger had left. He looked — dependable, but it was up to her now. She had to be strong and dependable for Billy's sake.

Bitter Disappointment On Arrival

The first class passengers disembarked in leisurely style, porters carrying their luggage, portmanteaux, hat boxes and large trunks, all man-handled down the gangplanks as the passengers strolled across the yards to waiting cabs and carts. Several splendid new motors were lined up further along the quayside. A crowd of people were gathered below the ship, some already waving to passengers lining the ship's rails.

The sun's rays began to penetrate the cool dawn air illuminating the busy scenes on the docks. Polly took a deep breath of the new country's air. On board she'd learned Australia was eight or ten hours ahead of England. The voyage over, she thought of Charlotte Street; it would be dark and cold, Annie fast asleep in bed, maybe dreaming of Donald Nightingale, or maybe the new café. Her father? How was he coping without her? She longed for family contact and she'd ask Mr Potter immediately how she could contact her family. For the first time since she'd left England she felt a pang of homesickness.

Billy nudged her. 'Polly, when do we get off the boat?'

'Very soon. It looks as though all the first class passengers are off . . . '

'Look, down there on the quay, that man who was in first class, and on the train.' Billy waved, vigorously jumping up and down, 'Mr Peterson!'

'Shush, he can't hear you, Billy. Come along, we're moving, keep a firm grip on the cases — I've got money, letters and passport here in this bag, safely over my shoulder. Can you manage the suitcase?'

'Yes, but he's waving to us, Polly. See,' he pointed to one of the motors, 'golly, he's getting into one of the cars, speaking to the driver. Is it his car, do you think? He's coming out, do we wave, Polly? He's seen us.'

Polly reluctantly waved in the direction Billy was pointing and sure enough she glimpsed the dark head of Jack Peterson turned in their direction.

He smiled, waved, then moved on towards the immigration sheds.

'Must have a lot of money,' Billy said, 'if that's his motor.'

'Doesn't follow, he may be being met by someone rich. Anyway, do forget about him, Billy, just concentrate on looking after our bags.'

When the first class passengers were off it was everyone for his or her self. Billy and Polly were jostled good-naturedly along, everybody now anxious to be off the boat, many anticipating being met by friends or family to start their new life.

Halfway down the gangplank there was a hold up, someone had lost a piece of baggage. Billy jigged about impatiently, peering on to the wharf. 'Look, there he is again, and the older lady, she's seeing some girls on to a big cart, and the other woman, they're giving out food and drinks to the girls in the cart. What are they doing, Polly?'

'I've no idea. Now, we're moving at last. Look sharp.'

Five minutes later the two Fletchers stepped on to firm soil for the first time in forty days. 'Oo-er,' Billy stumbled, 'I feel a bit giddy.'

'It's all right,' Polly took his arm, 'you'll adjust in a few minutes, just as you adjusted to the ship's motion on board. Uncle Harry told me about it.'

'Look, the man's getting into one of those motors again, and he's waved off the cart. Polly, will I ever ride in a motor car, do you think?'

'Course you will, even one of your own one day, but there's a way to go yet,' she squeezed his arm, 'there's no knowing what the future holds, we'll just work as hard as we can. You can go to school too, and look, an omen, the sun's right out now. Isn't it exciting?'

There was a great deal of activity on the docks, tearful reunions, bewildered passengers, crowds of people making for the immigration sheds to form queues for processing. Uncle Harry had told her all new immigrants would be vetted and health checks carried out before they were allowed in. People not 100% fit would be refused entry, so they had both been checked by their Castlebridge doctor.

'Fit as a fiddle, sound as a bell,' he'd signed off Polly but frowned a little over Billy. 'Small for his age, needs to exercise more, but he'll be passed fit enough.'

Polly concentrated on finding her bearings. There were many ships in the harbour, mostly sail ships. The steamship, *Orient*, dwarfed most of them. She looked back at the ship with affection, she and Billy had been happy on the voyage and time had passed all too swiftly. Now they had to face the realities of their undertaking.

'Come along, Billy, let's follow the

crowd. Immigration sheds are over there, lots of people are going that way.'

Billy cast a longing backward glance to where they had seen Jack Peterson's motor car and the cart. 'Couldn't we go and speak to him?'

'Goodness, of course not. Whatever for?'

'Well, he said if we needed help . . . ' Billy cast an apprehensive look at the crowds ahead queuing at the immigration points.

'We don't need help, we just need to find Mr Potter as Uncle Harry instructed us. So, come along, let's join the queues. I'm sure Mr Potter will be waiting inside, and Billy, do watch our bags. There's such a crush here, hold on to them tight.'

Billy nodded, 'I am, look.'

'Good. Now let's find where to go.'

Half-an-hour later she had to admit the procedure wasn't as simple as she'd first thought. Once inside the large sheds queues snaked away from the several desks attempting to process the new immigrants. Twice Polly found that for a reason she couldn't fathom they arrived at the wrong desk to be told that they both needed a medical inspection before the entry procedure could begin.

'Men and boys over in that queue, you wait here, Miss. You'll be called.'

'Oh please, this is my brother, can't I go with him?'

'Well . . . ' the burly official looked at them both.

Polly pleaded, 'Please, let me go with him, we had checks back in England before we came. I've a report. Billy, let me have that small case.'

The official looked at his watch. 'Hurry up then, Miss, you can see we've a lot of people to get through before we close up.'

She found it difficult to understand his accent, it was more clipped than she was used to. 'Here it is, sir, our medical reports from England.'

The man ran his eyes down the two sheets of paper. 'Hello, what's this?

You're A1 yourself, Miss, but the lad — small for his age isn't he — nasty cough . . . ?'

'Oh please. A . . . a Mr Richard Potter is to meet us here, and my uncle, Mr Harry Fletcher, arranged it all.'

'Never heard either name, but you're in a different country now, different rules. Look, you seem a nice, good young lady, I'll pass you both through together. Into the medical tent, out of here and first left.'

'Thank you, sir. Come along, Billy, we'll find Mr Potter soon and it'll be fine.'

'I'm hungry, Polly, we didn't have breakfast.'

'Poor lad, he does look as though he needs feeding up,' the officer said sympathetically, 'there's a truck should be outside by now: hot drinks, soup, bread and cheese, courtesy of the Australian government.' He paused and looked kindly at Polly. 'Got a daughter just about your age, I shouldn't like to think of her arriving in a foreign country so far from home, and in charge of a boy, so best of luck to you. Off you go, next one please, step up to the desk.'

'Come along, Billy, quickly, let's get the medical done, then we'll have something to eat. Mr Potter should surely be here by now.'

'How'd we find him in this crowd?' Billy asked, his face anxious.

'Oh Billy, do cheer up and do trust me. I told you, it's bound to be confusing at first.'

The medical examination was swift. A smiling young doctor declared Polly 'fit as a fiddle' and 'a nice healthy young woman we're glad to accept into our country'.

She was allowed to watch Billy's medical check.

This time the doctor frowned. 'Billy Fletcher, quite fit but a nasty cough still. Needs to build up muscle. Is he going to school here, Miss Fletcher?'

'I hope so. I believe my uncle has arranged it.'

'Good. Best of luck to you both then.'

By this time Polly was hungry but there was still no sign of Mr Potter. She and Billy went in search of food.

There was a crowd around what described itself as a chuck wagon where several ladies were serving up mugs of tea, bowls of soup, and hunks of bread and cheese. 'Come along now folk, hot tea or soup, bread and biscuits, and welcome all to Fremantle, Australia — finest town on earth.'

There were a couple of unoccupied trestle tables and chairs close by the wagon. 'You sit down, Billy, over there. I'll bring the tea and bread.'

By the time she had the food and drink the crowd was already thinning around the wagon. A motherly looking woman was sitting next to Billy.

Billy sprang up. 'Polly, you've been an age.'

'Sorry, it took a long time.'

The woman smiled. 'Oh, Billy's been keeping me company. I'm part of the tea wagon brigade, 'Ladies from Fremantle Welcome Club'. We like to meet and greet new country men and women at the docks to give them a hand if they need it.'

'That's kind of you. I was getting a bit worried, I was hemmed in a bit at the wagon.'

'Well, you want to watch out dear, just the situation where you'd get your pockets picked or your bag snatched. Just be careful now.' She stood up. 'Anything I can help you with? It's my turn at the tea urn right now.'

'Thanks, but we'll be fine. A Mr Dick Potter is supposed to be meeting us, one of the mining company's men. He must have been delayed.'

'I don't know the name but then Fremantle's a growing town. Can't know everybody. I do hope he turns up soon, time's getting on, we'll be closing the tea wagon soon — mine's the last shift. I should go back if I were you, inside to the queues. It's easing off a bit, no more immigrant ships in now until tomorrow. I hope your Mr Potter turns up . . . oh . . . ' she rummaged in a large handbag, 'here, the name and address of our organisation, just in case your Mr Potter's been delayed. And there's the name of a couple of hotels in town, cheap but clean and wholesome. We vet them ourselves and they'll give you a good discount if you show them this paper.'

'Thank you. I'm sure we won't be needing it, but I certainly feel better to have it. It's very kind of you.'

'Not at all. We do what we can, most of us have been through all this too, some thirty years ago in my case.' She swept her arm over the dock, sheds and ships. 'Early days can be difficult but, my dear, it'll be worth it in the end, you'll see.'

'Thank you, you've been very kind.'

Polly couldn't help feeling a pang of loneliness as the woman disappeared into the chuck wagon. But she had the piece of paper and put it in her pocket just in case.

'Right, Billy, back inside to the queues, can't be too long now.'

But it was several hours before they were summoned for a final check at an immigration desk. The process was slowed and further confused by a section in the sheds where newly-cleared immigrants could find immediate employment. Fremantle ladies were looking for servants, house-helps, even nannies amongst the many young females from Britain. Thinking back, Polly wondered if the cart of girls she and Billy had seen leaving earlier were destined for Peterson households.

* * *

By late afternoon there were still many people milling around the sheds. Babies and young children were becoming fractious. Immigration officers, up since before dawn, looked tired. Polly had constantly asked if a Mr Richard Potter had asked for her. After so many negatives she was beginning to feel twinges of unease.

Eventually she was called to a desk. 'Miss Polly Fletcher of Castlebridge, England,' a weary-looking official frowned and sighed as though he longed for his day's work to be over.

'Yes,' Polly answered, 'a Mr Richard Potter . . . '

'So it says here, but he's not here, is he?' The man looked at her and then flicked through the papers in a file. 'Is he your sponsor?'

'Er . . . no, he's a friend of my uncle, Mr Harry Fletcher of Castlebridge.'

This failed to impress the official, and he sighed. 'Well, it's getting late, Miss. I hope he gets here soon. Do you have somewhere to go from here?'

'No . . . but . . . he's bound to come.'

'We'll be closing up in an hour or so, and you can't stay here.' As he picked up the papers a bearded man who'd been sitting on a nearby bench went up to the official and spoke softly to him. The immigration officer looked at Polly and Billy and said something Polly couldn't catch. Billy, back on the bench was drooping after his early morning start.

'Right, Miss Fletcher, I'll just do a final check here then you can wait for this Mr Potter to arrive.'

'Thank you, I'm sure he'll be along any minute.' She noticed the man who had spoken to the official had gone to sit on the bench next to Billy.

'Mmm,' the immigration officer leafed through her papers, 'everything seems to be in order here . . . ah . . . ' he paused and looked again first at Polly, then Billy. 'It says here the boy's health record is not quite up to scratch and he has a criminal record, been in a juvenile prison for six months — for stealing. We have a problem here, Miss Fletcher . . . '

'But . . . my uncle . . . it's a sort of charity scheme. He fixed it so . . . '

'Fixed? That's against our rules — not a word I like.'

'It's a special scheme, my uncle and Mr Potter, he's got letters sponsoring us, me and Billy.'

The officer took out a fob watch. 'We're closing very soon. If this Mr Potter doesn't turn up you'll have to go back to the ship. I can't let this young fellow in without proper authority.'

'But . . . but what shall I do?' Polly's heart sank.

'You can go on, but the boy will have to stay here. We have special cells for doubtful entrants.'

'But he can't stay here on his own . . . '

'I can't let him in and it's a possibility we may have to send him back to Britain.'

'No! That's impossible, you can see he's no criminal,' Polly turned around. 'Billy? Where is he?'

'Young lady?' the man who'd previously spoken to the immigration officer came up to the desk, 'see, over there by the door . . . '

'Billy!' Polly yelled and made a dash towards her brother who was struggling with the heavy door. An officer left his desk nearby and took hold of Billy who tried to twist out of his grip.

'Billy hold still, I'm coming,' Polly ran to her brother's side. 'Sorry,' she gasped to the man who was holding on to him, 'he's just a bit scared. All this, it's so strange.'

'We don't want any trouble, Miss, just go back to the desk where you were at and the officer there will deal with you.' He gave Billy a shake, 'You just behave yourself, we don't want trouble-makers here in this country.'

'He's not a troublemaker. He's only eleven.'

'That's no excuse,' the official said sternly.

Polly held on to Billy with a firm grip. 'Billy, don't do that again, please.'

'He's going to send me back to prison. I want to go back to the ship. Polly, don't leave me.'

'Course I won't, you silly, but just keep quiet, say you're sorry first though.'

'Sorry, sir,' mumbled Billy as they

returned to their original station where there were now two officers.

Both looked sternly at Billy. 'Now young man . . .'

'He's very, very sorry. He's just . . . well, he's just tired and frightened. Please, I'll take care that he doesn't do it again.'

'It's all a bit of a mix-up here. My colleague says you're waiting for a Mr Dick Potter.'

'Yes. He has a mining company. I've papers in the name of the company.'

'Well, he's not shown up.'

'Can't I telegraph my uncle in England?'

The two men conferred and were joined by the man who had been sitting next to Billy on the bench.

Polly strained to hear what they were saying as they kept glancing, first towards her, then Billy. Finally the officers nodded, one left to go back to his own desk, the man on the bench remained. He was thick-set, bearded, well into middle-age, his weather-beaten face furrowed into a frown.

The official spoke to Polly. 'Well, Miss, it doesn't seem your Mr Potter is going to show up. Now, I can't let you into our country without a sponsor, but it just happens that my friend here, Bert Hackett, a farmer, is looking for some help in his household and on his farm. It's not unusual for farmers and mine owners to come down here when immigrant ships come in to offer employment once they've cleared immigration. Now, I can let you and the lad into the country if Mr Hackett is willing to sponsor you, which he is . . . '

'On condition you come along with me right now, Miss,' the farmer spoke.

Billy edged closer to Polly and grasped her hand.

'Well, that's very kind of . . . er . . . Mr Hackett, but that's not possible. My uncle . . . '

'Yes, yes, we've heard about your uncle and this Mr Potter, but they're not here are they? And the officers are closing up any minute. I'm a family man,' Bert Hackett said gruffly, 'wife and son at home. You've no fears.'

'But I can't possibly just come with you, all the arrangements are made for me.'

'No sign of that,' the officer said sharply. 'Now, this has gone on long enough, I'm shutting up shop, you can't stay here, and I'm in two minds whether to arrange for the boy here to be shipped straight back to where he's come from.'

'No, no, Polly . . . ' Billy's voice shook.

'Not much of a choice,' the farmer said. 'I'll see you both right. If we set off now we'll be home before midnight. I've got a truck outside.'

'No. No thank you.' Polly suddenly remembered the woman from the chuck wagon. She fumbled in her pocket for the paper the woman had given her, then remembered it was in her bag. 'Look, I have an address here and a hotel where we can go. Once there I can contact my uncle.'

'Afraid not, Miss. Can't risk it without a sponsor. If . . . '

'Billy, where's my case?' Polly's heart lurched. 'You were looking after it — under the bench. Billy! Where is it?'

'I . . . I . . . when he said I had to go back to prison I . . . I ran off. Oh Polly, it's not there now, somebody must have stolen it.' He began to cry.

Polly closed her eyes, counted slowly up to ten, and exhaled before looking directly at Bert Hackett.

'Mr Hackett, I don't know a thing about you. How do I know I can trust you? And I'll have to go to the police about my bag; my papers were in it, and all my money.'

'Police'll never catch who's got it — too many thieves coming into our country,' the immigration officer frowned.

'My offer's genuine,' the farmer said, 'I admit I'm desperate, but I need someone to help at home. My wife's not well, and there's a lot to do on the farm. Young lad here'll have to set to.'

Polly put her arm around Billy. 'He'll work hard if he's treated fairly, but we shan't be staying long.'

'We'll see how you suit.' The farmer was evasive.

'Look, there are people still waiting to be processed,' the immigration officer spoke sharply, 'and I need to get home to my wife tonight, not tomorrow morning. So, there's your chance, Miss Polly Fletcher, either you go off with Mr Hackett here right now, I can vouch for his integrity, he's a lay preacher at his local place of worship. You could do a lot worse . . . seeing as no one's claimed you yet . . . and I'm still undecided about your young brother. Seems to be the sort of troublemaker we don't want here. So, if you're not going along with Mr Hackett here I'd just as soon return young Billy Fletcher to the land of his birth.'

There was silence, broken by Billy's whispered plea. 'Polly, let's go with the man, don't leave me.'

'Don't worry, I'll never leave you alone.' She turned to the farmer. 'Mr Hackett, I'll come with you as a temporary measure on one condition . . .'

'You're not in a position to make conditions, Miss,' the officer frowned.

'No,' Mr Hackett held up his hand, 'fair's fair, she can have her say.'

'Can you help me contact my uncle in England? I can leave your farm once he's sorted things out for us.'

The farmer paused for a few seconds. 'Oh aye, I can do that, but you might like it on my farm, you might even want to stay. It's a great place, fresh air, home produce and you and the lad can have a nice room.'

Polly couldn't see any way out, with money and papers gone, and threats to Billy which she had no way of knowing could be carried out. She had to agree. She was a stranger in a foreign land, but she would learn as fast as she could how to adapt, how to fit in, and gradually make a new life for herself and Billy. One thing for sure, she wasn't going to settle for long at Mr Hackett's farm whatever it was like.

'All right, Billy, we'll go along with the gentleman, see how we like life in the real countryside.'

'Good on yer,' Bert Hackett produced a thin smile, 'you won't regret it. Let's go.'

Polly Feels Trapped

The immigration officer stamped the official seal on Polly's papers, shuffled the rest of the paperwork together, took a final look at her passport which also had Billy's details. As she reached for her passport Bert Hackett snatched the papers from the officer and tried to take Polly's passport too.

'My papers, Mr Hackett, please,' she managed to take her passport.

'Best I keep them for now, you're a bit careless with your things. I'll take your passport too.' He was already stuffing the papers in the capacious pockets of his farm jacket.

'I'll keep my passport, thank you.' She put it into her blouse, safe next to her heart.

'I've a safe at Mimosa Homestead,' there was a wheedling note in his voice.

Polly ignored it. Mimosa! Bert

Hackett didn't look like a man with a ranch named Mimosa.

'The missus — Sarah, took a fancy to it. Now, let's get moving, there's a long drive ahead.'

'How long?' Polly was already doubting the wisdom of her decision to follow Bert Hackett, but she really had no choice. Billy's eyes were fearful as he held tight to her.

'Few hours if all's well,' Bert replied. 'Got any tucker with you?'

'Tucker?'

'Food, water; anything from the chuck wagon.'

'No. I thought we'd have been away long ago . . . Mr Potter . . . '

Bert rolled his eyes, 'If he exists,' he muttered.

'I need to go to the police station.'

'You've got your cases?'

'Yes, but my money, papers, letters of introduction were all in the stolen bag.'

'Too late now. Sort it out back home.'

Home rang hollowly to Polly, though she supposed Australia was her home now, but as for Mimosa Homestead, that remained to be seen!

'My truck's over there, outside the immigration office.' Bert led the way to a large parking lot.

'Has he really got a car?' Billy whispered.

'Car?' Bert chuckled, 'not many over here have got a car yet. I'm a poor farmer boy, that old heap over there's our transport, at least it's motorised,' he pointed to a dusty truck with an open back piled high with sacks and boxes. 'Lad can hunker down under those sacks, not a lot of room up front.'

'No, Billy stays with me,' Polly was sharp, 'I'll go in the back with him.'

'Hang on to your door handle,' Bert shouted to Polly, 'sometimes drops off. Wouldn't want you to fall out after I've gone to all this trouble.'

Once clear of Fremantle Bert pulled into a trucker's stop. 'I'll get some water, you'd better come too.'

'Billy's nearly asleep, I'll stay with him.'

Bert scowled. ‘Don’t think for a second of running off . . . ’

She laughed. ‘Where’d we go, Mr Hackett? We’re entirely at your mercy.’

‘Right. See you don’t forget that,’ he stamped off, taking care to lock his door.

Polly looked around the parking lot — a few old motors, carts of all shapes and sizes, mostly old but a few newer ones. None as sparklingly luxurious-looking as the one Jack Peterson had approached. As she thought of him she felt a flutter of regret; if only he hadn’t left the immigration office she was sure he would have helped in a more positive way than Mr Hackett was helping them.

Billy stirred against her and she tightened her grip. ‘Don’t worry,’ she whispered, ‘we’ll be all right, just as long as we stick together. Think of it as a big adventure.’

Bert Hackett came hurrying across, unlocked his door and handed Polly a box. ‘Water, a few biscuits. Should be something at the ranch.' He went back to crank up the engine and scrambled back into the cab.

'Next stop, Mimosa,' he grunted, and didn't speak again until several hours later.

Polly had dozed a little, Billy had slept through the journey, but as the truck slowed to a stop near a huddle of low buildings he suddenly jerked awake.

'Polly — where . . . ?'

'We've arrived I think.'

'Where? I can't see the ship.'

'A long time since the ship, Billy. We're at Mr Hackett's ranch.'

Bert put his hand hard down on the horn which unleashed a frightful cacophony.

'Come on, you lazy devils. Colin, that you?' Dogs barking, snarling, leaping, flashes of white fangs! 'Down, you devil dogs. Don't mind them, as long as I'm here they won't eat you. Shut up,' he yelled. The barking subsided to a low growl. 'Colin, bring that light here.

We've got visitors. Is your ma all right?'

'Asleep, Dad, if the dogs didn't wake her.' The figure behind the lantern came nearer and Polly made out a tall form as he held up the light. 'Dad! What? Who . . . ? It's a woman and a boy. Why's she here? Is she another nurse. Is Ma that sick?'

'No, she's not a nurse. They're just off the ship at Fremantle. From England. Bit of bother with er . . . her papers. Wouldn't let the boy in so I offered to help her out in exchange for some work here, give a hand in the house, look after Ma when Mabel can't come.'

'They're staying? Here at Mimosa?'

'That's the plan. Let's get inside, is there food?'

'Mabel made some soup before she left.'

'Good. Inside, Miss Polly. Colin'll show you . . . I'll check the cattle.'

Colin continued his scrutiny of Polly, and she smiled tentatively. He jerked his head towards the house.

Billy hung back. 'Do we have to stay here?' he whispered.

'We do, just for a while. Food and shelter, Billy.'

They followed the bobbing lantern through the doorway which led into a large room, fireplace and range at one end, a long trestle table in the middle, with lighted oil lamps. Wooden stools under the trestle and a couple of rockers by the fireplace were the only furnishings.

The man, Colin, hung his lantern from a hook in a central ceiling beam. He came nearer to Polly and now she could see his face: tanned, bearded, long hair, dark eyes, watchful. Mid 30s Polly guessed. He still peered at her intently, ignoring Billy.

'Hello Colin,' she tried not to sound nervous.

'Hello.' He stepped away from her and touched Billy on the shoulder. 'Your son?'

'Gracious, no. Billy's my brother.'

'You're going to stay here?'

'Just a short while. Your . . . er . . . father has said we can stay and work. I need to contact . . . ' but Colin had turned away to the fireplace where a large pan sat on a trivet. He turned towards them. 'Soup? Sit down. Bread and cheese.'

Polly sat down motioning Billy to join her. The room was warm, the soup smelt delicious.

Colin filled two bowls and pushed a platter of bread towards them. 'Eat now.'

They didn't need a second invitation. Colin watched, never once taking his eyes off Polly. 'More?'

'Thank you, no. That was good.' There was something odd about Colin, she couldn't quite put her finger on it, but after the soup she felt exhausted and Billy too was drooping.

There were several doors off what must be the main heart of the house. Their cases with their clothes in were in the back of the truck. Colin Hackett was sitting at the table still watching her.

'Er . . . Colin, our luggage is in the truck and where shall Billy and I sleep tonight?'

'You're staying here?' He sounded surprised.

'Why, yes, your father told you.'

Colin beamed. 'That's good. I'll fetch your things.'

Bert Hackett came into the room carrying their two cases. 'You show them, I'm going to see Sarah.'

'She was asleep the last time I looked,' Colin said, 'I made her a hot drink.'

'Good lad,' Bert nodded approval. 'Bath house is outside, Miss Polly, but you'll not need it tonight. We only heat up the water now and then, washhouse is next door where there's a copper. Your boy's job will be to collect the kindling and you'll both have to be up before dawn — I'll make sure of that. There's plenty to do at Mimosa, we're not a luxury hotel.'

'Thank you, and thank Colin for the lovely soup.'

Colin looked startled by the compliment. With a glance at his dad he picked up the cases and went quietly out of the room.

'Mr Hackett, when will I be able to contact my uncle in England?'

'We'll sort that out when you've worked your passage here.'

'But . . . but my papers and money?'

He shrugged. 'You've no option, Miss. When I'm ready and next going into Fremantle, we'll see about it then.' He turned his back on them and sat down at the table. 'Good night,' he said, and started on his soup.

The room Colin Hackett took them to was small and windowless with rush matting covering the earth floor, but there was a fair-sized bed with plenty of rough woollen blankets and pillows. Tired out, Polly and Billy were asleep within seconds and perhaps it was fortunate for Polly that she couldn't hear the late-night conversation between Bert Hackett and his son, Colin.

* * *

It was still dark when Polly woke to the banging on the door. 'Polly Fletcher, get up. I expect breakfast on the table in fifteen minutes and you, Billy, get dressed right now, there are the animals to see to. I'll show you what to do.' A final bang on the door and he went clumping down the corridor.

'Hurry, Billy, just do exactly what he says. We can't afford to cross Mr Hackett.'

'All right, I'm dressed. I'll go out right now and don't worry, I'll look after you.'

'Oh Billy, love!' she pulled him to her and planted a kiss on his forehead, 'that's the spirit, we'll get out of this, don't you worry.'

Bert Hackett and his son were sitting at the table with mugs of strong tea. 'There's the teapot,' Bert pointed, 'needs a refill, scullery's out back. There're eggs and bacon in the cool house. Breakfast in ten minutes. You

Billy, come with me and take note because you'll be doing what I tell you on your own tomorrow, and just you remember, you don't ever get fed before the animals.'

House-keeping, cooking and providing was second nature to Polly and in minutes she found provisions, coped with a calor gas bottle and cooked bacon, eggs and some cold potatoes she found in a wire-netted safe. She kept a portion back for her brother.

'How's your wife, Mr Hackett?' she asked as she laid the plates before the two men. Shall I take some breakfast to her?'

'She'll only take tea and maybe some warm bread and milk. Get your own breakfast now. Colin, you stay here and show Miss Polly over the rest of the house.'

'Dad, I have to see to the animals.'

'I'll manage that, along with Billy. You just get acquainted with Miss Polly, take her to see your ma later. Oh, and you'll have some help for an hour or two this morning. Mabel Brown's coming in — she does a few hours a week. Mebbe we can cut her hours now you're here, Polly Fletcher.' He stood up. 'We'll be out all day, we'll need food bringing out to the fields. I've rustled stuff for today, and we'll need a hot meal tonight. There's stuff brought from Fremantle.'

'But I must contact my uncle in England, he'll be worried sick. Please, Mr Hackett, I'm willing to work hard for our keep for a few days but I must get to Fremantle to telegraph . . . '

'I've told you, in good time. Don't pester,' he snapped his fingers at the dogs lying by the door, 'come on boys, time you two were working.'

'But . . . '

'Miss Polly, don't be sad,' Colin said hesitantly, 'we'll get you to Fremantle but you've got to stay here first. We have to do as Dad says. I'll take you to see Ma now.'

'Shouldn't you be out in the fields too?'

'Not today. Dad said to look out for you.' He touched her hand gently, 'I'll go outside when Mabel comes.'

In a surprisingly large and comfortable room Mrs Hackett was propped up with pillows, eyes closed, breathing heavily.

'Ma,' Colin touched her shoulder lightly. Miss Fletcher, Ma . . . ' he turned to Polly, 'where've you come from?'

'England, Castlebridge,' she added automatically.

Mrs Hackett nodded, with a faint smile, 'Nice to have you here. It's too much for Bert, you'll stay I hope.'

'Well . . . I . . . '

'Yes,' Colin said quickly, 'she's staying.'

'Good. Now let me sleep. Is it Mabel's day today?'

'Yes, Ma.'

She closed her eyes and they tiptoed out of the room.

Mimosa Ranch itself was spacious — several large rooms, some full of junk, some partly furnished. Colin followed Polly like a small dog until she could stand it no longer.

'Please, Colin, why don't you go outside, I'm sure there's lots of work to do. I can manage here, I need to check out the provisions your dad brought back from Fremantle.'

'Dad said . . . ' Colin looked worried.

'But we don't always take notice of Dad do we, Colin?' a voice boomed behind him.

'Mabel,' Colin turned round.

'That's me. Mabel.' A large broad-hipped woman came into the room. 'What you got here, Colin? A young woman?'

'Dad brought her and Billy off the ship at Fremantle.'

'Ah, one of them. I told him I could manage. You're not having my job, Miss, we're managing well enough without extra hands, and who's this Billy, another mouth to feed?'

'I've no intention of taking your job, truly. I've got to go to Fremantle, my bag was stolen at the immigration office with all my papers and money. I'd no option but to come with Mr Hackett when he offered us shelter.'

'Hmm, we'll see. From England, eh? I've heard about you immigrants. Not scared of hard work are you?'

'I've looked after my family in England since my mother died nine years ago and I had a job too, in an office.'

'I see. Perhaps we'll get along then, you'll cheer the place up a bit. I'll be glad for you to do the cooking. Larder was low the last time I looked. I'm a nurse, my main job's Mrs Hackett but he . . . Mister . . . tries to get me to do the lot. So I'm glad you're here, Polly Fletcher.'

'Is Mrs Hackett very sick?'

'Let's say she's not likely to be doing much more cleaning and cooking. Mr Hackett is devoted to her.'

'How long has she been ill?'

'A couple of years bedridden, never a strong woman. It's a hard life out here and Mrs Hackett wasn't used to it. She came from the city you see. Bert Hackett swept her off her feet, built this ranch house for her — as you see he never properly finished it, and once Mrs Hackett took to her bed . . . ' she shrugged, 'things have gone further downhill.'

'That's a sad story.'

'Even sadder when Colin came along.'

'Sadder? Why?'

'Colin's not quite . . . how shall I put it? He's remained like a child. Oh, he's strong as an ox but . . . his dad worries about him all the time, and of course what'll happen to the ranch when he and Mrs Hackett are gone?'

'Gone?'

'Dead. Dead and buried. You must see the problem, a successful farm needs a dynasty of strong ones to keep it going. The boss has workers of course on the ranch, but it's not the same and it's family that you want to pass on the fruits of your labours. Right now there's no-one to pass Mimosa Homestead on to.'

'I see, but Colin may marry one day surely?'

'Colin! Marry! Fat chance, this is a new country, still pioneering, and still mostly men. There's a real shortage of women in spite of your country sending shiploads out. Ah, I think I see . . . ' she stopped abruptly, 'no, sorry, what a fool prattling on. I must go to see my patient, Mrs Hackett and you should be checking the stores. Men'll need refuelling in a few hours.'

'Yes, but why did you suddenly stop — about pioneers and women?'

'Nothing, not my place to say. I don't know Mr Hackett's plans, I may be wrong . . . '

'There's something isn't there, something you're not telling me?'

'I don't know you.'

'I'm Polly Fletcher from England and I must get to Fremantle to contact my uncle. Mr Hackett seems reluctant to help me.'

Mabel sighed. 'I should learn to keep my big mouth shut, but seeing as you're from England, that's where my parents came from, emigrated here in the early days.'

'But you know something about the situation here.'

Mabel was silent, then shrugged. 'Well you'll find out soon enough, if I'm right.'

'You're worrying me. Mabel?'

'All right. Mr Hackett's tried this before. Only the once — it didn't work out.'

'What didn't work out? Please. I've my brother to look after.'

'Young lad I saw with Mr Hackett?'

Polly nodded.

'Ah. Extra bonus — cheap labour. Look, I must go and see my patient.'

'Please, tell me.'

'I really must go to Mrs Hackett. Go and check the stores, get the men's lunch ready then brew up some tea and I'll talk to you then. Sun's shining, we can sit out back. Mrs Hackett tried to make a bit of a garden years ago but it's all gone to seed now. Still, it's a nice sunny place to sit.'

Polly busied herself in the back kitchen bagging up lunch for the men and preparing the evening meal. She found loads of supplies in a sort of cold room off the kitchen.

Mabel soon came back and Polly carried a tray of tea and biscuits to what she could see was once a pretty garden.

'You've done well. All done, you deserve a little break.'

'Mrs Hackett all right?'

'Yes. Had her medicine and went straight off. Isn't this sun lovely?'

'Yes it is, but tell me . . . you stopped . . . you've something to tell me.'

'I should never have said a thing but . . . oh lord . . . what a dilemma.'

'Please.'

'All right. Now, you've met Colin and you know he's like a child in a man's body.'

'Mr Hackett . . . he manages to keep afloat, the money doesn't worry him, it's the ranch's future that does. It's become an obsession to pass on Mimosa. Sadly they lost two babies before Colin and after Colin, Sarah Hackett couldn't have any more children.' There was a pause while Mabel drank more tea, and cast a side-long look at Polly. 'Now do you see?'

'Er . . . no . . . sorry. I can't see that it affects me and Billy. I just want to contact my uncle in England.'

'And I bet Mr Hackett has stalled on that one.'

'Well, yes, but it's early days, we only arrived yesterday.'

'And no word about going to Fremantle — your lost papers, money, contact with home?'

'No, but . . . '

'Miss Polly, I see I have to spell it out to you. It's quite well known in these parts, don't think Mr Hackett hasn't tried locally . . . '

'Tried what? Please . . . '

'To find a wife for Colin. There, I've said it. Now do you see?'

'But . . . but that's ridiculous.'

'No, it's not. Not for Mr Hackett, and I'll lay a bet he'll even include Billy in the package if the lad fits in to ranch life.'

'Marry Colin Hackett? He can't force me, we must leave right away.'

'He'll find ways to keep you, and the community will be on his side. They won't help you, I'm afraid. Life here is often a fight for survival and family tradition is very important.'

'Surely there are a lot of young women in the area . . . '

'Would you like to be married to Colin Hackett?'

'No, but . . . I've got Billy to think about. He has to go to school. I have an office job lined up in Kalgoolie at my uncle's mine.'

'You're better off than most then. Maybe I was a fool to tell you.'

'Oh no. I'm grateful, I just can't think how I can get away. I don't suppose you could contact my uncle in England?'

'Me? No. I want to keep my job here. I shouldn't really have told you but at least you're forewarned.'

Automatically Polly sipped her tea, if what Mabel had told her was true, and she felt in her bones it was, she had to get away from Mimosa Homestead as soon as possible. But where to go and how to escape were huge problems. All she had was some loose change that she'd had in her pocket at immigration.

The only plus she could see was that at least she had her passport, but how soon before Bert Hackett found some method of stealing it from her and destroying it.

An Unexpected Meeting

The following days ran into weeks as Polly tried to focus on a plan of escape but her brain was dull, devoid of ideas, and it was hard to grasp the enormity of her position — moneyless, helpless and friendless. So it was perhaps fortunate that she was sucked into a daily hard work routine — that, at least, she could cope with.

It was in her nature to work hard and she quickly adapted to the programme — up before dawn, breakfast, mugs of tea for the ranch hands, food out to the field at noon, supper to prepare, tidying, sweeping, washing, cooking. Dog-tired at day's end her brain blanked out, fast asleep in seconds, as was Billy.

It was one consolation to see Billy swiftly adapt to farm life, he loved working with animals and had a natural ability, earning praise from Bert Hackett.

'We'll make a farmer of you yet, young man.'

'I'm afraid we won't be staying that long, Mr Hackett,' Polly daily reminded him she had to reach Fremantle.

Bert fobbed her off with excuses. 'Truck's not working. Too busy this week. I've a town meeting.'

Town was a handful of dwellings and an all-purpose grocery store and garage along a dusty street. Polly had never seen 'the town', and her only female company was Mabel and Sarah Hackett. Sometimes in the evening she would sit with Sarah Hackett who loved to hear Polly talk of her family and life in Castlebridge.

Polly found these visits calming and therapeutic, space for her brain to grapple with the problem of an escape plan.

Colin Hackett, when not in the fields, followed Polly around with a dog-like devotion. She felt sorry for him, but tried to avoid him.

For several days the routine was unbroken, then one evening Bert Hackett called Polly into a cluttered little room he called his office. Colin smiled, Polly's heart sank.

'Dad's something to say to you . . . ' he paused, then in a rush, 'and you do like me . . . a bit, Polly?'

'Well, you've been very kind to Billy and me, but we can't stay here much longer. Colin, you must know we have to leave. My Uncle Harry will be making enquiries when he doesn't hear from me.'

'Oh . . . but . . . ' his eyes were puzzled, 'Dad says . . . ' he shrugged, 'he knows what to do. I think I'll go and find Billy. He's in the stables, he loves horses, don't he?'

'He does.'

'And you're talking to Dad now?'

'I believe I must.' Brain racing, heart thumping, Polly went into Bert Hackett's office. 'Mr Hackett?'

'Polly, sit down, sit down. I'll shift

these papers — file 'em one day. Mug of beer?'

'No thanks, Mr Hackett.'

'Bert, Polly, please. I feel we've got to know each other a bit these last weeks . . . ' he coughed, 'it's . . . um . . . good to have you here.'

'Thank you, Mr Hackett, but you know I have to contact my uncle . . . '

'Yes, yes, but there's no need . . . '

'He will be worried. He's sure to contact the immigration office.'

'But you must stay here,' he interrupted quickly, 'can't you see Colin's grown very fond of you. I know he's a little — shy, but your sons would inherit a good prosperous farm and . . . '

'Mr Hackett! What on earth are you talking about? Sons? That's . . . ridiculous.'

'You could do a lot worse.' Now he was scowling, his large hand taut on his mug of beer, 'and I don't see you've much of a choice.'

'But surely you can't keep me here against my will. And Billy . . . '

'Billy's happy here, you can see that.' He banged his fist on his desk, 'and I don't want to hear one more word about this uncle. If he was interested in your whereabouts we'd've heard by now.'

'There hasn't been time, but surely you don't want to force me to marry Colin?'

'That's exactly what I do want, and folks around here will support me. Sons are vital to this country so you just make up your mind to being Mrs Hackett junior as soon as I can make the arrangements.' He paused. 'The alternative is to turn you and Billy out and I warn you, you wouldn't last long out there. It's a wild place for a penniless lone female.'

'But . . . '

He held up his hand. 'No buts, fate brought you to Mimosa Homestead and here you'll stay. Got it?'

Polly clutched the arms of her chair. Suffocating anger, panic and fear made her feel sick. She stared at Bert Hackett but his eyes were as hard as steel, obsessed with his plan, determined to have his own way. She couldn't win this fight, the odds were stretched against her. It was a desperate situation needing desperate measures. Only one way, she and Billy must escape, but she must seem to agree to his bizarre proposal to gain time.

She took a deep breath. 'Mr Hackett, you've given me a shock, give me time, let me think. Billy does appear to have settled, but Colin, I hardly know.'

'Someone else? A boyfriend back in England?'

'Er, well, no . . . just give me a little time to think about your . . . um . . . proposition.'

'No point in waiting. I'll be setting the wheels in motion tomorrow.' He began shuffling papers on his desk. 'That's all, you can go now, and perhaps you'd look in on my wife before you go to bed. I've a lot to do here.'

Polly usually did look in on Sarah

Hackett when the day's chores were over. Sarah enjoyed her company and never tired of talk of England. Tonight she sensed Polly's unease. 'Something wrong, Polly dear?'

'Er, no, well, yes . . . it's difficult. Mr . . . '

'My husband?' Sarah sighed. 'I can guess, my husband wants you to marry Colin.'

Polly gasped. 'How did you know?'

'I don't miss much, lying here, and my husband confides in me. Polly, he's not a bad man, but he has an obsession and it's almost an illness now. My illness is physical, his is mental, an obsession, a crusade to have his grandsons at Mimosa.'

'But I can't.' Polly said desperately.

'Of course you can't, and it wouldn't be right. You must contact your uncle.'

'I've already asked many, many times.'

'I know, and I should like nothing better than to have you and Billy stay here, but my husband has grown bitter with disappointment with no sons but Colin to carry Mimosa forward into the future.'

'But I can't marry Colin,' Polly repeated tearfully.

'I know, I know, it's impossible. So, Polly, you and Billy must run away, get to Fremantle . . . '

'Bur Mr Hackett . . . '

'Won't come after you, I'll see to that. He'll be coming to sit with me soon, come back tomorrow evening and I'll have a plan. Talk to Billy, he's a good boy, soon old enough to look after you.' She spoke slowly now, tired out. 'Go now, Polly, no-one can buy a family.'

Polly had little sleep that night while Billy was dead to the world. He had grown up in the few weeks at Mimosa and he seemed settled. Perhaps for the sake of her young brother she should marry Colin Hackett and provide a secure life for Billy. This would be a better life than the one threatening Billy if he had to go back to England. Dawn was just breaking as she fell into an uneasy sleep.

The morning brought more trouble and Mabel came in early to tend Mrs Hackett. She was full of excitement. 'Polly, you're a dark horse, keeping it so secret.'

'What?'

'Why, you and Colin getting married. It's the talk of the neighbourhood — Mr Hackett's dream come true.'

Polly was silent.

'Ah, so it's true.'

'Er, not entirely. Now, I've lots to do this morning.'

Mabel shrugged. 'All right by me as long as I still have a job here.'

'Oh, I'm sure you will have.'

Somehow Polly got through the day. All the men were out on the ranch until dusk and Mabel left early. Polly made a small bundle of their belongings and waited for evening — they'd have to leave most of their luggage behind.

At supper Colin was subdued, Polly fearful and anxious — only Bert was in a good mood. 'All settled then. We should celebrate.'

'Billy's tired out and so am I.' Polly started to clear the plates.

'Oh well, we'll postpone celebrations. Maybe tomorrow.'

'Maybe. I'll say goodnight to Mrs Hackett first.'

'Of course. You're practically family now.'

Sarah Hackett was waiting for her. 'Mabel has told me Bert has already announced your coming marriage to Colin.'

'I'm afraid so. I don't know what to do.'

'You must go tonight, Polly. I have a plan.'

'But where, and how? I've no money . . . '

'I have money, you mustn't worry about that. Tonight's a full moon, wait until the house is quiet and the dogs asleep.' She took an envelope from under her pillow. 'This should get you to Fremantle, I have a friend there, her address is on the envelope. She will help you contact your uncle in England.'

'But Mr Hackett, won't he be angry with you?'

Sarah smiled. 'I can manage my Bert, don't worry. He has this dream of fine boys inheriting his land but he knows in his heart he would be wrong to force you into marriage. Don't blame him too much.'

'I'm so grateful to you, but promise no harm will come to you.'

'Of course I promise, and if it's any consolation it's happened before and we've survived, but I am afraid Bert may do the same thing again.'

'It's strange, but in some ways I'm sorry to go. If only Mr Hackett would have let me contact my uncle . . .'

'Never mind. Just be safe.'

'I'll send back the money.'

'Don't worry about it, but I should like to know what happens to both you and Billy.'

'Of course. I'll write.'

'Go to bed as usual tonight, perhaps

let Billy sleep for an hour or so then leave as quietly as possible. Take the track which leads you to the road and about two miles along the road there's a track on the left which widens into an old trail the Aborigines made years ago. Follow that trail for a mile or so to a camp used by sheep drovers and miners on their way to the outlying mines and farms. There is always someone there, coming and going, stocking up the camp with provisions. From there you should be able to find someone to take you on to Fremantle.'

'Mrs Hackett, I can never thank you enough.'

Sarah smiled. 'Maybe one day, if I can get well again, we shall meet.'

'I hope so.'

'One more thing, at the end of the Aborigine trail, several miles farther on there is a big ranch, our nearest neighbour, but their spread is much bigger than Mimosa's. A lady lives there, Caroline Peterson, she helps young female immigrants sent to

Australia from Britain to avoid the pitfalls of exploitation, abuse from employers, and enforced marriages which I'm afraid are not unusual. She will help you,' she took Polly's hand, 'take care, and good luck. I shall miss you.'

'Me too,' Polly took her hand, 'and thank you again.' She hid the envelope in her pocket as Bert Hackett came into the room.

'Still here? Isn't my wife well?'

'I'm sorry, Mr Hackett, my fault, talking . . . '

'Excited about the wedding, I expect. Never mind she's almost asleep now. Goodnight, Polly.'

'Goodbye, Mr Hackett.' Polly, making sure she had the envelope well hidden, quietly left the room.

An hour later the house was silent, and Billy was sound asleep. With a pang Polly noticed how he had filled out the few weeks they'd been at Mimosa Ranch. He was sunburned, his shock of hair a lighter colour and altogether a very changed boy from the pale, sullen, scared boy she'd seen in prison. The outdoor life suited him and as she watched him her heart sank at the prospect of uprooting him to an uncertain future. Was she doing the right thing?

He stirred and opened his eyes. 'Polly, is it time to get up?'

'No, love. Shush, we're leaving Mimosa.

'Why?' He sat up, eyes wide open.

'Because Mr Hackett will make me marry Colin if we stay.'

'Oh. And you don't want to?'

'No, Billy. I can't, I don't love him, and we have to go to Fremantle and contact Uncle Harry.'

'I like it here, Polly.'

'I know, but . . . '

'I wouldn't want you to marry Colin. I mean, he's all right, but . . . '

Polly hugged him. 'It wouldn't be fair, so we have to go now, but very quietly.'

'Do you know the way?'

'I hope so. We have to walk to a camp.'

Billy swiftly dressed. 'Will we know anyone out there?'

'Probably not.'

'Don't worry, I'll look after you.'

'Thanks, Billy, that makes me feel so much better. Quietly now,' picking up her bag, leaving most of their clothes behind she opened the bedroom door. Bright moonlight slanted into the homestead. Gentle snores came from Sarah and Bert's bedroom. They crept along the corridor, the big back door was locked and bolted. She carefully turned the key and slid back the bolts. Noiselessly they moved out into the yard, past the sheds where the domestic animals slept and within a few minutes were clear of the farm buildings.

She breathed a sigh of relief. 'Now down the lane . . . ' as she spoke there was an outbreak of yapping and barking as a couple of large dogs came racing after them, teeth bared, tails lashing furiously. She tried to suppress a scream, the first dog had her skirt in his teeth and was shaking it, practically ripping it.

'Shush,' Billy said sharply to his sister before turning to the dogs, speaking quietly but firmly, calling their names. At once the dog let go of Polly and sidled up to Billy and lay down at his feet. 'Good boys,' he touched the dogs' heads and instantly they sat quietly watching him.

'Billy! How on earth . . . ?'

He grinned. 'They're my friends, they work in the fields with us.'

'I hope they haven't woken Mr Hackett.'

'I shouldn't think so, we're the other side of the house.'

Suddenly dark clouds scudded across the moon, plunging the road ahead into darkness. Polly couldn't help a gasp of alarm. 'How'll we see?'

'Don't worry, the dogs will come along with us for a while, certainly until we get used to the road. Then I'll send them back.'

'Goodness gracious, Billy, I'm glad you're on my side.'

'Course I am. Always will be, you're my big sister.'

Polly was glad Billy and the dogs were with her, the darkness persisted, only glimpses of the moon lit up their path but it was a wide road, well used. She just prayed there would be no other users before they turned off on to the Aborigine track.

Billy sent the dogs back after the first mile. Polly was sorry to see them go, but she and Billy set up a good pace and soon reached the turn-off to the track which would lead them to the camp.

'I hope so,' Polly said, more confidently than she felt.

'Don't worry,' Billy took her arm, 'it's getting light. See?'

They walked on, past some smouldering ashes and shapes of tents loomed ahead, a long wooden shack behind the tents. They stopped. There was total silence until, probably sensing their presence, horses stared whinnying; snorting, shuffling. That set the dogs barking, men began emerging from the tents, bleary-eyed with sleep, rubbing their faces and beards.

'What in all the world . . . ?'

'Who the . . . ?'

'It's a woman — and a lad.'

'What on earth . . . ?'

'Please,' Polly called over the clamour, 'we're travellers on the way to Fremantle. Can we rest here a while?'

'Where've you come from?' A young man stepped forward.

'Mimosa Homestead,' Polly said quickly.

'Hackett's place?'

'Yes.' Polly wished she hadn't said anything, they were bound to tell Bert, maybe keep them there until he came for them. 'Look,' she said desperately, 'there's a note from Mrs Hackett. I have to get to Fremantle.'

Quite a crowd had now gathered, curious to see the visitors. An older man brought out some wooden boxes and blankets. 'Let them rest a bit,' he said to the crowd, 'they look dead beat. Brew up some tea, find some manners amongst you.' He put the blankets on the boxes and Polly sat down thankfully.

'Who's the boy?' the man asked.

'He's my brother. We're from England.'

'England! Er, you're far away then, from home?'

'We are, but we must get to Fremantle. I've work there.'

'Long way from Fremantle, Miss. We're all going in the opposite direction — to the pastures, and some of us to the gold mines. This is a transit camp for the farm and mine workers.'

'What? No-one's going to Fremantle?' Polly asked desperately.

'Here ye'are,' a stooped old man brought tins and mugs of tea and hunks of bread.

'This is Pete,' the younger man said, 'he sort of runs the camp. Lives in that shack over there. Know anyone going in the Fremantle direction, Pete?'

'Not that I know. Workers generally go in t'other direction this time of the year.'

'Can we stay here for a while?' Polly asked, 'I've a little money here. Maybe . . .'

The younger man shook his head. 'It's not really suitable, we're all moving on today. Only old Pete for a day or so. Oh . . . ' he stopped, 'I know, the boss could help, he's due any time now, maybe turn up today. Take a chance on it, rest up a bit, I'll scout around.'

'Cheer up, Poll,' Billy nudged her, 'we'll be all right, you try to sleep a bit, I'll keep an eye open.'

'Aren't you tired?'

'Not a bit. It's an adventure.'

'Good,' Polly yawned, 'that's the spirit.' She closed her eyes and was asleep in seconds, oblivious to the din around her. She dreamed they were back in Castlebridge, Billy was in court, in the dock, all her family were there. George, her father, Annie, with her Donald, Uncle Harry, Victoria, even baby Wilfred. The magistrate addressed Billy . . . 'banished from here, transportation never to return to England for one hundred years'.

'No, no, please,' Polly rushed to take Billy, in her dream she had wings, lifted him up. There were shouts and yells and clapping which woke her.

'Miss, Miss,' someone was shaking her, 'The boss, he's here.'

'Wake up Polly,' Billy's excited voice, 'you'll never guess. Look, look, he's here, it's the man on the train, on the boat — Mr Peterson, he's the boss here.'

Polly And Billy Find Refuge

Polly rubbed her eyes and blinked. It wasn't a dream, the man in the train, the man on the boat, was actually standing above her. She remembered his dark-blue eyes, which were astounded at his discovery. She tried to scramble to her feet, conscious of her appearance, her clothes were crumpled, her face and hands unwashed. She tried to smooth down her skirts, tucked her hair behind her ears.

'Mr Peterson! How on earth . . . whatever are you doing here?'

'I could ask the same of you, Miss . . . er . . .'

'Fletcher, Polly Fletcher, and my brother here, Billy.'

'I remember. How do you do, Billy?' Jack Peterson offered his hand.

Billy shook it with a big grin on his face. 'I told Polly she should have spoken to you at the docks.'

'Hush, Billy.'

The man who'd spoken to Billy when they arrived stepped forward now. 'We couldn't believe our eyes, Boss. Woman and boy came wandering in just before dawn. Walked over from Mimosa, quite a trek.' He turned to Polly. 'I told you the boss might be here today. Your lucky day, I reckon.'

'Oh, I hope so. Please, Mr Peterson, can you help us? I have to get to Fremantle, nobody met us at the dock. Something must have happened, and Immigration threatened to send Billy back to England on his own. I didn't know what to do, then Mr Hackett . . . '

'Ah! Bert up to his tricks again,' Jack Peterson frowned, 'the immigration people should put a stop to it. I've a good mind to tell the police that . . . '

'Oh, please, no — my money was stolen and all my papers. Mr Hackett gave us food and shelter and Mrs

Hackett gave me some money and told me to come here where someone might be able to take us to Fremantle, and she mentioned Caroline Peterson, their neighbour. From there, I need to contact my Uncle Harry.'

'No problem,' Jack Peterson smiled. 'Caroline Peterson is my mother.'

Polly felt profound relief. 'Can you help us? Really?' Automatically she tried again to smooth down her hair, was certain she looked an absolute fright.

Jack Peterson's smile was even wider, his eyes warm. 'Of course I can. If only I'd spoken to you on the docks I could have warned you.'

'But I expected my uncle's contact to meet me. I can't imagine what's happened to him.' She felt as though a great weight had lifted from her shoulders — if only she could have a wash!

'I've got some work to do here first,' he said. 'I need to pay the men and give instructions for the coming weeks. Then we'll be on our way back to Four Seasons Acres.'

'Four Seasons?'

'The family ranch. It's a few hours away but we've got a cart so you'll be fairly comfortable. Do you ride, you or Billy?'

'No.' Polly couldn't help a smile — riding in Castlebridge indeed!

'I'd like to,' Billy said.

'And you shall. I'll teach you, we've plenty of horses at Four Seasons and you can stay while we find out what happened.'

'But . . . but your mother? Won't she mind us being there?'

Jack threw back his head and laughed. 'Mother? Mind? She'll be in her element. It's what she does, you see — sort of her crusade.' Before Polly could ask any more questions Jack had turned back to his men who had gathered round him. 'I won't be long,' he called back, 'over in the shack, there'll be hot food — and there's a bath house behind. Old Pete'll supply you with soap and towels.'

Polly had never been so thankful for a bowl of tepid rain water and a bar of rather gritty soap. She brushed out her silky hair. Her skin had been tanned by the Mimosa sunshine and it glowed.

'You look nice,' Billy was towelling his hair.

'I think we both look a bit tidier.' Polly combed her hair through her fingers, thanking her lucky stars again that Jack Peterson had turned up that very morning. After a meal of beans and potatoes brother and sister sat on a bench by the bathhouse and watched the buzz of activity in the camp.

Jack was everywhere: checking the work loads, dispatching workers to their various tasks, some to round up the sheep, others to the wheat fields. Finally the men lined up behind a makeshift desk to receive their wages before setting off to their workplaces. As they rode past Polly they waved and grinned. 'Good luck,' one or two called.

'Maybe see you at Four Seasons,' the

man she'd spoken to when they arrived called out to her.

Finally, around noon, most of the men had gone and Jack came to sit with Polly and Billy. 'Feel better now?'

'We do, thanks to the men here. They've been really kind.'

'We look out for each other. It can be a hard life — if the harvests fail or animals go sick it can be a disaster. This is still a very new country, Miss Fletcher.'

'Oh, Polly, please — and Billy and I don't want to be a bother.'

'You won't be, and it'll be good to show you a part of our new country.'

'But my uncle . . .'

'We'll contact him, but things can move pretty slowly sometimes, so we'll have to go to the telegraph office. Tell you what, Miss . . . Polly, Mother will be pleased to have house guests, especially ones from England.'

'Oh?'

'Ma is from England, me too, but that's another story. Right now we'll concentrate on getting to Four Seasons before nightfall. We might just make it.'

'Is it far away?'

'Well, the boundary's not far, but we're thousands of acres from the homestead.' He stood up. 'We'll make a start right away. Billy, you can ride up with me for a while, Polly, you'll follow in the cart. There's plenty of room now the supplies are out — and there are a couple of parasols. Joe'll drive and look after you.'

'Parasols?'

'Sun protection. I guess you spent most of the time at Mimosa indoors as a general cook and bottle washer,' he shook his head, 'I must really trek over there soon, have a word with Bert Hackett.'

'Oh, but Mrs Hackett was so kind. I promised to get a message back to her. She gave me an address in Fremantle.'

'We'll take care of that: Now, let's make a start.'

* * *

That day and the ride to Four Seasons Acres was Polly's true introduction to the vastness of Australia. At Mimosa, apart from the constant sunshine, she could have been back in Castlebridge, except that at Mimosa she was closely confined to the domestic role. Now, as the small party left the camp she had a bird's eye view of the surrounding country.

Evidently Jack Peterson was in mixed farming. Pastures of cattle grazed in enormous paddocks, then farther on, acres of wheat dominated the landscape. Scrubland lay between wheat and dairy, with eucalyptus trees breaking up the terrain.

Up front, Billy frequently turned around, excitedly pointing to some feature or animals.

'Roos, over there,' Joe pointed as he flicked the reins.

'Roos?'

'Kangaroos. Look, over there, family of 'em. See the babbies, joeys we call 'em — in their mothers' pouches.'

'Oh, yes. How sweet.'

'Yeah, well, they can be destructive. Proper scavengers.'

It was mid-afternoon before Jack called a halt by a small lake. 'Rest up here for an hour, feed and water the horses, stretch your legs. Billy, are you all right?'

'Yes, it's fun. Will I truly learn to ride a horse?'

'Of course. We'll go out on the ranch together. Would you like that?'

Billy's eyes were round with joy, 'Yes please. Please.'

'Billy, don't forget we're going to Fremantle to see . . . '

'I know, but . . . '

'We'd be happy to have you stay over at Four Seasons for a spell, see a bit of the new country. I'm sure Ma will do her utmost to keep you for a while. Once you've got in touch with your uncle.'

'We don't want to be a bother,' Polly shaded her eyes against the sun, loving its warmth on her skin.

'No bother. We love visitors, especially from England. Hey, you need a sun hat as well as that parasol, it's still summer here.' He rummaged in a box at the back of the cart. 'Here,' he pulled out a wide-brimmed straw hat and put it on Polly's head, tucking strands of her silky blonde hair behind her ears.

'Polly felt herself blush so moved away quickly. 'Thank you, Mr . . . '

'Oh, Jack, please Polly. You'll find it's not so formal here as back in England.'

Again Polly had to hide a smile, Castlebridge was hardly a hot bed of formal behaviour. 'This country's certainly different from what I've seen so far, not that I've seen much of it — only Mimosa ranch.'

'We'll have to put that right. The hat suits you — at least a touch of Aussie land.'

Again Polly felt that ridiculous fluttering of the heart as Jack touched the brim of the hat. She was glad her face was concealed by the wide brim.

'Grub up, Boss.' Joe had heated up

beans on the makeshift camp fire. Billy ate ravenously while Polly was content to munch an apple and enjoy the sun.

'Winter in England,' Jack commented, 'glad to miss out on that, I guess.'

Polly nodded. 'It's lovely to feel the sun, it's probably freezing back home.'

'Treat it with respect, it can be fierce. Sometimes we have to pray for rain, especially at harvest time. Can be pretty dry and dusty, you'll see,' he squinted at the sun. 'Best get moving, I'd like to get home before nightfall. Saddle sore, Billy?'

'Not a bit,' lied Billy.

'You'll get used to it.'

'Billy will be going to school as soon as we're settled. Uncle Harry's given us an address in Fremantle.'

'Schools have holidays, don't they?' Billy asked.

'Course they do. If you're going to be an Australian boy you'll have to be a good horseman.'

'I will, I will.'

Jack saddled up and helped Billy mount up behind him. 'Next stop, Peterson's Four Seasons.'

* * *

The hot sun was soporific and Polly's eyes closed, the missed sleep of the previous night caught up with her as the motion of the cart rocked her into sleep. An hour or two later she woke with a start.

'Miss Polly,' Joe called over his shoulder, 'just passed the boundary of Peterson's Four Seasons. Thought you'd like to check out the land.'

'Of course,' she struggled to sit up. 'We're nearly there?'

Joe laughed. 'Not quite, about another hour to the house.'

'Goodness. Must be a big farm.'

'Yep. Mostly are in these parts. One thing we've got plenty of here is land, acres and acres.'

'Er . . . what's in these fields?' town born Polly looked dubious at the green shoots dominating the landscape.

'Wheat here, but the Peterson's ranch has sheep too, and fruit orchards near the house. Bit of everything I guess, as well as all the females.'

'A big family, the Petersons?'

Joe laughed. 'You could say that, I suppose.'

'But . . . all female?'

'You'll see.' He shook the reins, made a peculiar clicking noise with his teeth and the horses increased their speed. 'They smell home you see,' Joe chuckled.

The sun was sinking as the small procession went through an open gate which led to a gravelled drive. Polly sat up and clutched the side of the cart. Tall eucalyptus trees lined the long avenue, their scent faintly carried on the evening breeze.

Joe pointed with his whip as the horses trotted eagerly forward, 'Almost there. That first building, over there, is for the females.'

'Females?'

'Yep. Pass it in a minute. They'll be at supper . . . ah, a couple there having a stroll,' he lifted his hand. 'Hi, ladies, a good day?'

'All right. Milly's gone though,' a tall girl replied.

'Aw, that's a shame. You were good friends, weren't you?'

'We still are. I'm hoping to join her in a few days. Who's this then?' Both girls stopped by the cart. 'A new one for us?'

'Not quite. House guest more like. You'd better be getting back to the building. Be dark soon.'

'All right,' the girls smiled at Polly, 'maybe see you later.'

Polly smiled back just as Jack and Billy cantered past them.

Joe shook the reins and followed them. 'There's the ranch house, just by those trees. I'll drop you there by Jack and Billy. I'll see to the horses.'

'Thank you so much . . . er . . . Joe, I've really enjoyed the ride.'

'Good. I'll be seeing you then.'

'Oh, but we . . . ' she turned round but he'd gone.

'Over here, Polly,' Billy, walking a little stiffly beckoned her towards a long, low wooden building with a verandah or deck running round it. 'That's their ranch,' Billy whispered. 'Come on, Mr Peterson said to come along to the house.'

'Where is he?'

'Just gone in. We're here, I suppose,' he clutched Polly's hand, 'it's exciting, isn't it?'

'I . . . um . . . not sure . . . there's nobody here.'

'Mr Peterson said to go to the door. Come on.'

Polly followed Billy. Dusk was falling, strange bird noises were coming from the dark wood near the house but the evening air was balmy. Now Polly clutched her brother's hand. 'Billy, are you sure . . . ?'

'Yes, come on — the front door, on the porch.'

Gingerly they climbed some wooden

steps on to the verandah, a screen door led into the house and as they hesitated, the door was flung open and a babble of noise startled the silent air.

'Please, please come in. Jack, how could you leave our guests out on the porch?' A tall dark-haired woman held out her hands. 'Miss Fletcher, and Billy, welcome to Peterson's Four Seasons Acres. I'm Caroline Peterson, do come inside.'

'I was just telling Ma your story,' Jack smiled, 'but everyone had so many questions.' He smiled. 'Sorry.'

'Well, come inside now, dear, and meet the family,' Mrs Peterson took Polly's arm. 'I'm afraid there are rather a lot of us, and then there are always one or two of the girls. The new ones are a bit shy when they first arrive, so we always have a family meal together.'

'Girls' thought Polly, puzzled. 'Was this some sort of school?'

'Didn't Jack explain?'

'Er . . . I don't think so. Something

about immigrants, er yes, Sarah mentioned . . . '

'Yes, young girls from England, and Ireland too. I meet them off the boat at Fremantle . . . but I'll explain later. We'll have supper now.'

Mrs Peterson led the way into a large kitchen with a long table in the middle. To Polly the room seemed very crowded, mainly young girls though she spotted Joe sitting at the table. Mrs Peterson clapped her hands.

'Everyone, this is Polly and her brother, Billy, from England. If you'll all sit down we'll have supper and I'll introduce everyone.'

Nods, smiles, and a scraping back of chairs on the slate floor as Mrs Peterson went round the table. 'My daughters, Hannah and Mary, cousins, Sam, John and Peter — they work on the ranch. Joe, Jack's right-hand man, you've already met.'

The list seemed endless and Polly knew she'd never remember all their names . . . 'and finally, our neighbour,

Helen,' she smiled affectionately at a pretty dark-haired young woman sitting next to Jack. 'One day soon we hope Helen will be part of the family too, don't we, Jack?'

Jack put his arm round Helen's shoulder. 'Sure do. Once our two farms are in one family we'll have the biggest spread in the neighbourhood. Makes sense, Helen?'

'Mmm,' she nodded, smiling at Jack in a way that made Polly's heart plummet. But what on earth did she expect? Jack Peterson, handsome, confident and assured was obviously on the way to becoming a rich landowner by marrying his sweetheart.

Polly concentrated on counting her blessings. She had by chance stumbled on kind and good people who would surely help her to contact her uncle and set them on their way to Fremantle. She smiled across the table at Billy who was tucking into supper and talking animatedly to the boy next to him.

After supper the girls cleared up

while Jack and the men went out to settle the animals and plan the next day's work in the fields. Jack was soon back.

'Ma, you'll look after Polly and Billy, I've a stack of paperwork to do — lots to catch up with since I've been away.'

'It's good to have you home again, Jack, it seems so long . . . ' she turned to Polly, 'he's been in England for six weeks. We've all missed him so much.'

'In England? Of course, he was on the boat, you too, Mrs Peterson. Billy and I were on the *Orient* too.'

'Really? Why didn't we see you?'

'We were cabin class. But we loved the voyage.'

'What a coincidence — and that you should end up here.'

'Well, I should be in Fremantle but . . . '

'Yes, Jack's told me. So sad. At Mimosa? I'll have to call on Sarah Hackett.'

'But it's such a long way.'

Mrs Peterson laughed. 'Not really,

you get used to it, I travel a lot looking after my ladies, which reminds me I should check on the dormitory.'

'Dormitory?'

'The large hut — as you come in. Would you like to come with me?'

'Yes I would . . . but what . . . ?'

'I'll explain as we walk along, and don't worry about Fremantle. Jack's sure to be going that way in a day or so and then we can telegraph your uncle. We don't have electric phone lines here yet, but progress is on the way. There are a few disadvantages to living off the beaten track.'

Billy had already gone off with Joe to look at the animals and the supper visitors had gone to their respective beds.

Mrs Peterson took Polly's arm. 'The ladies in the dormitory are girls who have either emigrated by choice or who have committed fairly minor crimes in England and are looking to make a new life in Australia. Unfortunately they are often exploited, sent to unsuitable work places where they run away and that's usually where trouble starts. Peterson's Four Seasons Acres is a place of refuge for girls who can't settle or find employment. I help them to find jobs in respectable houses, or stores, or even find suitable husbands if that's what they want.'

'Oh, of course, Sarah Hackett mentioned it.'

'Don't be shocked, Polly, there's a shortage of women here, the country needs young families. I try to acclimatise the ladies to life here.'

'Aren't you from England?'

'I was, but now . . . here we are, let's say goodnight to the ladies.'

Oil lamps cast a soft glow in the room where there were a dozen or so beds with side tables and a chair. One or two girls were chatting quietly, some were already in bed.

'Ladies,' Mrs Peterson clapped her hands, 'this is Polly Fletcher from England. She'll be here for a few days with her young brother, Billy. Maybe she'll come with us on our next placement trips before she has to go to Fremantle.'

The women nodded, some spoke to Polly as Mrs Peterson went from bed to bed, talking to the ladies. One or two younger girls were quiet, very sad looking. Mrs Peterson sat on their beds, took their hands in hers, and spoke softly to them before finally straightening their bed covers and bending to kiss them goodnight.

'All well, ladies,' she asked, 'any problems or worries please tell me. I can probably help. Sleep well, see you in the morning. Maybe we can take a picnic down to the river, show Polly and Billy what a good place this is. Goodnight ladies.'

'Goodnight,' Polly echoed quietly.

As they walked back across the yard the moonlight shrouded the fields and bushes, night animals rustled in the undergrowth, the air was balmy, warm on Polly's face and she breathed a sigh of relief. Peterson Acres was a good place to rest awhile.

'Thank you, Mrs Peterson.'

'What for?'

'Oh, making me welcome, taking us in . . . '

'Nonsense — a pleasure to have you. I'll double up a room for you and Billy, we've lots of room here but we also have plenty of visitors too. Will that be all right?'

'It certainly will, Mrs Peterson.'

'Oh, Caroline please. Australia's much more informal than England.' She sighed. 'I have the ranch in Australia but sometimes I long for just a touch of the homeland.'

'Where was that?'

'In the north of England — York.'

'Goodness, I'm from the north too — Castlebridge.'

'What a coincidence, but I've been here a long time. You're still thinking of . . . where . . . Castlebridge? As home?'

'I did to begin with, but now I don't know. So much has happened.'

'And I'm sure a lot more will happen before you get to Britain again.'

'If I ever do,' Polly sighed wistfully.

'Sure you will, the story's only just beginning for you, Polly. I feel it in my bones.'

'Hope so.' But Polly couldn't erase the image of Jack Peterson with his arm lovingly round someone called Helen.

Contact With Home At Last

The next few days at Four Seasons were the happiest Polly had spent since arriving in Australia. The homestead was a happy house with family members coming and going at all times of the day. She helped clean and cook and Billy was out on the ranch from dawn until dusk.

By the end of their first week she swore he was well on the way to becoming a real Australian, there was even little sign of his northern English accent.

Hannah Peterson, Jack's older sister, taught at the small local school and one morning Polly went with her to talk to the children about England.

'You're a natural,' Hannah said as they went home, 'have you not thought about teaching?'

'Well, no. I'm a book-keeper, but anything's possible. I suppose, in a new country if I get to stay — maybe.'

Between them Jack's sisters had fitted Polly out with enough clothes to last the summer. 'We keep a trunkful of cast-offs for the immigrants too, some of them are in a pretty bad state by the time they arrive here,' Hannah told her.

Polly spent time too with Caroline Peterson and her 'ladies' preparing them for the trek to their possible placements within the next week.

'I hope you'll come with us, Polly,' Caroline Peterson said, 'the ladies have got used to you and it'd be a great help to me.'

'I'd love to but . . . my uncle, I should contact him to tell him we haven't forgotten.'

'Ah yes, I know Jack wants to talk to you about that, he was looking for you earlier on. Tomorrow's his Fremantle day, I believe.'

'Oh,' Polly couldn't help a pang of

disappointment at the thought of possibly soon leaving Four Seasons.

'It shouldn't take you too long, we're this side of Fremantle, Jack'll take the cart and he'll be picking up supplies, but he'll take you to the telegraph office first. Do your folks have the new electric telephone?'

'No, but my uncle does. He has a big department store and office in Castlebridge.'

'So you'll be able to talk to him?'

'I hope so, that'd be wonderful. I'm really worried about my dad, and why there was no one to meet us at Fremantle Dock.'

'That must have been very frightening. Jack tells me we were on the same boat, what a shame we didn't meet.'

'It was Billy I was worried about, he . . . ' she stopped, not sure whether she should tell Mrs Peterson about Billy's criminal record. Later, maybe, when they got to know Billy better.

'I do hope you'll stay with us for a while. It would be such a help to me, and Billy's taken to the ranch work as though he'd been born here.'

'I'm glad, but it will be hard to tear him away.'

'Perhaps you won't have to, let's wait and see what the news from England is. Now, if you've time to spare I'd be glad of some help with my paperwork. You did say you were a book-keeper in Castlebridge?'

Polly nodded. 'I'd be pleased to help.'

'I have to keep a record of the ladies' placements and expenses, the church and other charities help fund me so I must keep track of them for a while and I'm not the best record keeper in the world.'

Polly picked up the work very quickly and Mrs Peterson was glad to leave her in the tiny office at the back of the ranch house. Immersed in the task of sorting out finances and checking placements for Mrs Peterson's ladies, Polly was startled when Jack came in.

'Polly,' he smiled, 'just the person. Fremantle tomorrow?'

‘Oh, that would be kind,’ Polly tried to avoid Jack’s eyes and made herself frown as she looked up at him.

‘All right, Polly? You don’t look too pleased. I thought . . . ’

‘Oh I am, very pleased, it’s just . . . just . . . well . . . er . . . ’ she floundered and stumbled. Although she was very worried about her family in England the spell of Peterson’s Four Seasons was becoming a beguiling temptation.

‘So . . . ’ Jack frowned, ‘an early start tomorrow. Five a.m. too early for you?’

‘Of course not, I’m used to an early start.’

‘That’s fine then.’ He held her gaze for an unnerving long time before turning on his heel and abruptly walking away.

Polly bent her head to Mrs Peterson’s somewhat irregular accounting but her heart was in turmoil as she acknowledged she must leave Four Seasons as soon as possible to avoid a broken heart.

* * *

Next morning she was reconciled to whatever the trip to Fremantle brought. It was a beautiful dewy summer morning and she was determined to enjoy her day out with Jack Peterson — probably her last!

'Ah! You're bright and early,' Jack brought the horse and cart to the front of the ranch.

'I expect you've already done a day's work in the fields.'

He laughed. 'Well, a bit. It's a busy time of the year.'

'I've brought a picnic,' Polly climbed up beside him, 'your mother organised it.'

'She's a great organiser, is Ma.' He flicked the reins, 'would you like to try your hand at driving?'

'Oh no, thanks. I've no idea how . . . '

'It's easy. Maybe on the way back. Sit tight, the horses are a bit frisky early morning.'

Polly tied her sun hat more firmly on her head as they rattled along the farm track to the road. She was conscious of

Jack's body so close to hers on the narrow driving seat.

The horses moved along briskly and soon the rural countryside gave way to straggles of ranch-type houses and a couple of stores.

'You've already been to Fremantle of course,' Jack said as the straggle of dwellings gave way to tall buildings, shops and several churches.

'Only the docks. It was dark when Mr Hackett drove back to his ranch.'

'It's a growing town, a lively port and . . .' He pointed with his whip, 'see that large grim-looking building which dominates the town? That's Fremantle jail.'

Polly shuddered, imagining Billy incarcerated there. 'I have an address in Fremantle, Mrs Hackett gave it to me.'

'Do you want to find it?'

'Well, maybe, I'll write when I have news from England.'

'I'm hoping you'll be staying with us for a while yet.'

Polly kept silent . . . if only!

'Here we are, the telegraph office. We'll telegraph first, then try the telephone at your uncle's house. He'd be home from his business now probably. Early evening in England.'

'Please. It's very good of you.'

'Not at all, I'm just as intrigued as you are. Your entry into this country was a pretty bad experience. Do you want to call at the police station about your stolen bag?'

'Do you think it's worth it?'

'Probably not. As Fremantle grows so does petty theft and crime, but it wouldn't do any harm. Let's contact England first.'

Fortunately Jack Peterson was well known at the telegraph and post office as a frequent caller to England. A clerk promised to put a call through to Harry Fletcher's house, and took Polly's letters for franking.

'Special delivery Miss, take a good few weeks otherwise?'

'Oh no, I can't afford . . . '

'Special delivery, please,' Jack interrupted quickly.

'Oh no, please,' Polly tried to take them back. 'I've no money, Jack, I can't even pay for my keep.'

'Don't worry, Ma will give you plenty of work to do, and she'll pay you of course.'

'Oh dear, I don't . . . '

'Your call's through, Miss, a Mr Harry Fletcher on the line,' the clerk called.

'That was quick,' Polly was shaking with excitement and apprehension as she picked up the receiver. 'Uncle Harry, Uncle Harry . . .'

Crackle, crackle, then a faint voice. 'Polly, Polly, is it really you? Where on earth are you? We've been worried sick. I've tried everywhere. Immigration, your dad . . . '

'Is Dad all right? Annie . . . ?'

'Yes. Just worried to death.'

'I'm . . . we're both fine. It was . . . hard, but now I'm at Four Seasons, Peterson's ranch.'

'What?'

'A ranch, Uncle . . . ' the line faded and crackled. Polly looked imploringly at the counter clerk.

He nodded, fiddled with the machine and Harry's voice came back.

'Polly . . . ?'

'I'm well, and Billy is wonderful. He loves it here but we've no money. It was stolen, but people here are so kind to us . . . '

'Oh Polly. I'll send you a money order right away.'

'Thank you so much. I'll pay you back of course . . . '

'Please, Polly, forget it. You're in Fremantle now? Are you staying there?'

'No. We're on a ranch a few hours' ride away. What should I do, Uncle, and what happened to Mr Potter who was supposed to meet us?'

'It was dreadful . . . he . . . his mining company went bankrupt, I've lost a lot of money I had in it too. He committed suicide, Polly, a few days before your ship was due to dock. I didn't find out . . . ' There was a lot more crackling and static, then faintly, 'a job for you still and school for Billy. All fixed . . . the telegraph details to Fremantle . . . pick up . . . will write, express . . . address . . . '

'Uncle, I can't hear you.'

'Telegraph Office . . . so relieved to hear you're both safe, Polly love . . . ' and with a final static burst the line went dead.

Polly tried to swallow back the tears pricking the back of her throat; if only she could see them all, her dad, Annie, Uncle Harry and his family, and suddenly a sense of desolation swept over her.

'Polly,' Jack was immediately by her side, 'are you all right? Let's go outside, it's stuffy in here, get some air. Thanks,' he called out to the clerk who'd managed the phone call. Outside the air was balmy, soft and warm. He tucked Polly's arm in his. 'There's a café down the street with a garden. You must be hungry, we'll have some food — give you time to feel better.'

'I'm sorry, Jack, what a fool. It was just . . . they're so far away, and all that's happened. But I am truly grateful for what you and your mother have done for us.'

'Our pleasure. Here's the café, I don't think they do English breakfasts yet but the pies are just wonderful. A great Australian speciality.'

'I feel better already. I'm sorry to have been such a fool.'

'Not surprising you should be upset. Does your uncle have plans for you?'

'He's sending money, and I think I have a job in one of his businesses here — book-keeping I suppose.'

'And Billy?'

'School, I imagine. Uncle's sending me a letter by telegraph.'

'Good. They'll bring it out to the ranch.'

'Poor Mr Potter. He was the man who was supposed to meet me. He committed suicide, his mine went bankrupt.'

'That's tragic, the gold rush isn't what it was, the alluvial mines are running out, so many people are turning to wheat, dairy products and fruit.'

'Jack Peterson, good to see you again.' A smiling young woman gave Jack a hug. 'Who's your friend today?'

'Lucy! This is Polly Fletcher, from England. She's staying a while with us at Four Seasons. She's just contacted her folks and is now starving. Any decent tucker?'

'What a cheek. Course there is, best breakfast out. Go into the garden, a nice shady spot by the pines. Shan't be a tick.' She turned to Polly. 'My great grandparents came over from England — original settlers.'

'Are — so you're . . . ?'

'Australian through and through and proud of it. I'll be back soon with the grub.'

'Do you know everyone around here?' Polly laughed.

'Not quite.' He leaned back, tilted his

chair, closed his eyes and turned his face to the sun. Polly stared at his tanned skin, the strong planes of his jaw, his mouth — quickly she turned away as he brought his chair down to earth. 'What?' he folded his arms.

'Er . . . nothing. Just . . . um . . . sunburn . . . ?'

'You're right,' he picked up his bush hat from the ground and put it on. 'I'd almost forgotten about the sun while I was in England.'

'What were you doing in England?' Polly moved on to safer ground.

'This last time?'

'Mmm, you came back on the *S.S. Orient*.'

'Yes. I was born in England, parents were from the north, same as you. They moved around a lot, Dad was in the army. They lived in India, then Dad retired to Australia, sadly died soon after. Ma took the reins, moved to Four Seasons and became the female immigrants' friend. That's about it.'

'Do you visit England a lot?'

He nodded. 'My grandparents live in London. I spent a lot of time with them when I was little, I like to go back, I love London and I love Australia. I'll probably take Australian citizenship but my heart, my spirit, is still in England. Maybe when I settle down and have a family they'll be Australian and so shall I.' He leaned forward and took her hand. 'And you, Polly, do you think you'll be able to say you're Australian one day?'

His touch was warm, strong, healing. 'I don't know, it's too early.'

'What about your family? You've a younger sister, Annie, isn't it? I couldn't help overhearing.'

'Yes. I do miss her but she's going to be married to her Donald. Oh,' her hand flew to her mouth, 'I shall miss the wedding, shan't I? I never thought, how dreadful . . . '

'You might be able to go back for it. Is it soon?'

'I don't know, that's the problem. I feel so out of touch.'

'It's natural to feel that way. Any other sisters, brothers?'

'Oh, yes, Sam and Fred, but it's too sad. They came to Australia a couple of years ago. Dad had letters, money and then nothing. He assumes they're dead. Uncle Harry's tried to find out what happened but no luck.'

'Polly, you mustn't give up, especially now you're here. Once you're settled you can make enquiries . . . '

'But . . . so long.'

'Polly, a year is nothing in these circumstances. Were they planning to farm?'

'No. They went for the gold, Uncle Harry gave them money. He has interests in some mine but he said just now he'd lost money.'

'But there are lots of mines still operating. Your brothers might have gone anywhere and it's a wild country, difficult to communicate, hardly any transport. What are their names?'

'Sam and Fred Fletcher. Do you really think they may be alive?'

'They could be. They could have had an accident. Were they miners in England?'

Polly nodded. 'Yes, but pay and conditions were so bad they wanted a better life. A man from Australia, Kalgoolie I think, came to Castlebridge looking for experienced miners. Sam and Fred were so pleased to be picked.'

'Polly, give me any details you can think of, better still I could maybe telegraph your Uncle Harry and see what he turned up. I know the area, I can start things moving. That is if you agree.'

'But of course. Thank you so much.'

'Is there anyone you've left behind, someone who'll follow you out here one day?' His eyes held hers, his touch tightened, Polly wanted to cover his hand with hers, she reached . . . and then remembered — the happy smiling face of Helen, the neighbour.

'Oh maybe one day,' she lied. Fortunately breakfast arrived and the mood was broken.

* * *

Polly Fletcher's true nature was to make the best of things and she'd been doing just that since her mother had died leaving her to keep the family together. Circumstances had led her to a foreign land and she was going to make the best of that, for her own sake as well as Billy's. And there was much to observe in the rapidly growing town of Fremantle. Jack had to go to the store to buy both for the domestic Four Seasons home, and new supplies for the camp near the Aborigine trail where Polly and Billy had stopped.

Mrs Peterson had entrusted Polly to buy supplies for her 'ladies' in the dormitory and also for her next trek up to the bush to settle her girls into various placements in the outback.

Jack went to a farm supplier to haggle over some new equipment for Four Seasons while Polly browsed among the clothes stores, making a mental list of things she would buy if and when she had her own money. They met back at the telegraph office around noon to start back to Four Seasons, first picking up some more food from the café where they'd had breakfast.

Lucy gave them both a big hug. 'Come again soon, hope you stay around, Polly. Australia is great, you'll see.'

Polly laughed. 'Yes I am beginning to see. Thanks.'

Jack and Polly walked to the stables to pick up the cart and horses. The heat was quite intense, the sun at its peak. 'Maybe we should wait a while,' Jack said, 'it'll be cooler in an hour or so.'

'I'm fine. See, sun bonnet?'

'It suits you. All right then, once we're out of town, I think my next big buy will be a proper motor car, the roads are improving all the time.'

'I think the horse and cart or trap is lovely,' she climbed up beside him.

'It's a novelty for you, but think of the time a motor car would save.'

'I wouldn't see the countryside so well.'

'You win, but we'll stop in a couple of hours, have some food.'

Once well clear of the town the roads were quite rough and Polly began to see the logic of Jack's argument, though she did see kangaroos, unfamiliar birds and other small animals. She wondered if they were possums.

'Water hole ahead,' Jack called out, 'trees, shade, food.'

It was a small copse on the edge of a vast sea of yellow wheat which seemed to stretch to the far blue horizon.

'Goodness,' she breathed, 'what a sight!'

'Mmm. Part of the wheat belt runs right into Four Seasons wheat fields. You probably didn't notice it coming in, sun and sky bring it to life.'

'It's wonderful.'

'Hard labour, Polly, and unpredictable. One heavy rain season and your crops have gone. That's why we have some dairy too, but that needs water.

It's all a bit of a tight-rope and that's why I like to keep my options open in England.'

'What would you do there, and wouldn't you miss all of this?'

'Course I would, but neither would I want to be a bankrupt farmer. Just look on the bright side.'

'I try to.'

Jack paused as he released the horses. 'I think you do, Polly, and I admire you for it,' he put his hands on her shoulders.

Polly started and quickly broke free. 'Food, I'm starving.'

'Lucy's put in a feast. More pies, fruit juice and a wonderful fruit cake.'

'Lovely,' Polly sighed, leaned back against a tree, closed her eyes and fell into a doze within seconds. In a fleeting dream she was escaping from Mimosa only this time Bert Hackett was chasing her with his snapping dogs. Billy was nowhere to be seen, she called out to him, woke with a start and found herself propped on Jack's shoulder.

He turned his head, smiled, and kissed her.

Sleepily she kissed him back savouring the soft warmth of his lips. Then she remembered Helen! She pushed him away. 'Sorry, sorry, I was dreaming.' She stood up and shook out her skirts.

Jack looked mystified. 'Polly, what's the matter?'

'No, you shouldn't. I'm sorry . . . '

'Stop apologising. I only kissed you and I thought you kissed me back.'

'No, I shouldn't. Oh, let's get on to the ranch.'

'But the picnic . . . ?'

'Sorry, not really hungry.'

He stared at her, frowning, then began to pack up the food. 'If that's what you want . . . '

'Yes, yes, I do . . . and I'll ride in the back of the cart — more room . . . ' she tailed off. Jack was still watching her, still frowning. Then his brow cleared. 'Ah, so there is someone then. Back home?'

'Why yes. I expect he'll be coming to

Australia when we're settled.' She lied wildly, 'He's a teacher,' she said truthfully.

'You should have told me. I wouldn't have kissed you, I thought . . . we can still be friends . . . and I'll make enquiries about your brothers.'

'You've Got To Go To School'

Polly couldn't suppress a startled scream as a motor vehicle came speeding round a sharp bend in the track leading to the ranch house. Jack's yell was more expressive as he jerked the reins to halt the horses.

'What the . . . oh lord it's . . . what's the matter with him? You all right, Polly, I'm sorry I had to stop so sharply?'

'I'm fine but who was that? He looked furious about something.'

'A neighbour,' Jack said curtly, 'I think I can guess what he wants. I'd better get to the ranch house fast, we're almost there.'

The horses trotted quickly along the track towards the house. On the porch Polly saw Mrs Peterson and the young girl that she recognised as Helen.

'Blast,' Jack muttered as he jumped down from the cart.

His mother ran to meet him. 'Oh Jack, I'm so sorry you weren't here, Ken is in such a state. Helen rode over to warn us her father was livid . . . oh, sorry, Polly, did you have a nice day?'

'Yes thank you, I spoke to my uncle, Dad's well but worried and . . . '

'I'm sure, you must tell me about it later. Right now we have a bit of a family crisis. Helen has had a bit of a disagreement with her father, he's a widower you see, Helen's his only child, she and Jack . . . '

'Yes. Don't worry, I've plenty to do — if we're going into the bush from here for a while . . . '

'Oh yes, what a blessing, I'll be away for a while. Ken was . . . well, never mind. Now, stop weeping, Helen, Jack'll take care of you, and your father's anger rarely lasts very long.'

'But it's all so . . . ' Helen sobbed.

Jack put his arm round her shoulders. 'Shush, shush, it'll be all right. Stay here for a bit, I'll sort it out, calm down. I've got a horse that you haven't seen yet, bought him at the market last week, tell me what you think of him.' He kept his arm round her as he led her to the stables, talking softly. Polly heard him say quietly. 'Let's find Joe.'

Mrs Peterson stood on the stoop watching them, then with a sigh she turned to Polly. 'Families! Always something.'

'Why is Helen so upset?' Polly couldn't help asking.

Mrs Peterson had already turned away, calling over her shoulder, 'do come into the house. Polly, it's cooler inside, I want to check over the details of our trip, oh, and then we'd better see the girls, tell them exactly what's happening, then you must tell me all that happened in Fremantle.'

So Polly didn't find out why Helen was so upset. Lucky Helen, she thought enviously before she followed Jack's mother into the house. Fortunately there was much to occupy her as she and Caroline Peterson worked through the things they had to do for the trip.

Caroline ran her operation on a shoestring although she was supported by the church and various charities and she was becoming an important and well-known figure as she worked to provide good homes with families for her immigrants.

'You see, Polly,' she explained as she plotted the route to the various placements, 'my belief is that family life, family love, is a great natural force for good. That is why we try to place our young immigrants with families. Some of these poor girls have little experience of family love.' She handed Polly a list. 'Have a look at the itinerary, you should find it interesting. We'll camp out on a couple of nights just for the fun of it, the girls always love it, and we'll be away about four days. We'll go and talk to them now, but do tell me what happened in Fremantle today. You talked to you uncle?'

Polly told her what had happened

and that her uncle was still hoping to arrange both a job for her and school for Billy in Fremantle.

'Well that's good news for you but I'll be sorry to lose you, and Billy who is so well settled here. Would your uncle be very upset if you stayed here?'

'But I can't . . . '

'Of course you surely can if you wish. Billy could go to Hannah's school and you would be so useful in my work. We are setting up more depots in various towns for immigrant women. It's so important we settle them with suitable homes and jobs.'

Polly was silent, there was nothing she would have liked better, if only, but the thought of staying at Four Seasons and witnessing the happy union of Jack Peterson and his Helen was simply too painful.

'I expect my uncle will want me to follow any plans he has for us, though I've loved staying here,' she added hastily.

'Well, of course you must do as your

uncle wishes, but you know there would always be a home for you here and a job too. Now we had better go and brief my ladies.'

As they left the house and crossed the yard Jack came hurrying towards them. 'You're not off yet are you, with your girls?'

'No. Tomorrow, we're going over to them right now. How's Helen?'

'Better, a bit calmer. I'm going to see Ken later. She's with Joe now.'

'Joe?'

'Sure. He's showing off the new horse, you remember, the one we bought last week. Helen's putting him through his paces. He's a lovely animal.'

'Fine, but Ken will be . . .'

'Leave Helen's dad to me,' Jack cut in swiftly. 'Oh, and I'll probably stay over, especially if you're both away for a few days.' He turned to Polly. 'Can you leave me any details about your brothers, Polly, also your uncle's number in case I find anything out about them?'

'That would be kind. I've got some notes, places my uncle tried, and a couple of addresses we had during their first weeks here.'

'There was no reason they wouldn't keep in touch with their home, forgive me asking, but no family quarrels or disagreements?'

'No, they were always family-minded. At first they even sent money home, that's why we all fear something dreadful's happened.'

'Not necessarily. I told you Australia's a huge country and communications are difficult. Leave it to me, but don't get your hopes too high just in case. Have a good trip and take care.'

'Don't worry, Jack, Polly and I will take good care of the girls, and each other.' She gave her son a hug. 'Keep an eye on young Billy, and watch out for Ken's temper. You know he's only really concerned for Helen's happiness. He's a widower, Polly, and Helen's his only child so he's really keen that she and Jack . . . '

'Yes, Ma, I know all that. Let me handle Ken.'

'As you wish, dear. Now, Polly, those girls will be wondering where we are.'

Before she turned to follow Caroline Peterson, Polly watched Jack walk away, her heart heavy, knowing that unfortunately she had fallen in love with him, and thus it would be impossible to remain much longer at Four Seasons.

As soon as she heard from Uncle Harry and had some money she and Billy would leave. Meanwhile she would try to forget Jack and enjoy the experience ahead of her trip into the Australian bush. That would be a far cry from life back at Castlebridge.

* * *

Early next morning a score of excited girls gathered outside Four Seasons eager yet apprehensive to be on their way to the promised new life. Several were orphans, some had committed minor crimes, all were a long, long way from home, and some had made friendships on the voyage and at Four Seasons, so there was sadness as well as anticipation they would be parting from their friends and in all probability would never see them again.

Two horse-drawn carts carried them away from Four Seasons on a sparkly late summer morning. The houses and farms where Mrs Peterson had placed the girls were well out into the bush but the first property was a fine house at the end of an avenue of stiff symmetrical Norfolk pines. Here the first girl was dropped off to be a maid. Tearful farewells were obligatory but Emmie's eyes lit up as she was shown the cosy living quarters.

'Don't worry, Mrs Peterson,' the motherly woman in charge of the servants said, 'Emmie will be fine here, it's a happy household.'

Mrs Peterson bent to kiss Emmie. 'Work hard, be a good girl, and I will come and see you in three months.'

The group journeyed on and at every

inn or settler's home people came out to greet the travellers. One young girl was left at an innkeeper's. The innkeeper's wife knew Mrs Peterson well and as she stood at the door of the inn she put her hand on young Nellie's shoulder and called after the departing travellers, 'We'll find her a good husband. I'll see she doesn't marry a bad 'un.'

By mid-morning they had reached an inn where Mrs Peterson was also well known and the innkeeper's wife provided hot water for tea and gave them a midday meal of bread and mutton. Another girl was taken into their service.

As they journeyed on the day became hot and sultry, the pace of the animals slower, the farms were further apart. They stopped for a short break and the girls stretched their legs walking to a small stream. Polly went with them and they sat in the shade of some trees and dangled their feet in the water. The girls liked to hear about Polly's life in England, a couple of them came from the north of England like her.

'Why aren't you married, Miss?' one asked.

Polly laughed, she knew, to them, her great age of twenty plus put her firmly in the spinster category. 'Never met the right man,' she always replied.

'Maybe you'll find a man out here.'

'I'm not looking, I've got my brother, Billy, to look after.'

'Billy,' they exclaimed, 'he's a handsome young lad. Someone'll snap him up smartish.'

Polly was startled at the idea of Billy being 'snapped up', Billy was her little brother but of course he'd shot up since arriving in Australia, almost a teenager, and potentially very good looking too — outdoor work and the climate suited him. He would be snapped up, particularly in Australia where the men vastly outnumbered the women; a new notion for Polly, to be considered as a sort of elder spinster sister.

'Oh, but Billy's only a youngster.'

The girls laughed and nudged each

other. 'Hope I find one as handsome then,' a pretty young girl said plaintively.

* * *

At half past two they started off again and travelled for four hours before making camp for the night. There was a rudimentary shed similar to the one where she and Billy had met Jack Peterson but all the girls wanted to camp outside under the stars by a camp fire.

Supper was bacon sliced and fried with bread and large mugs of tea. The evening air was fresh, blankets were spread over the cart floors or placed over layers of dried leaves. They sat around the camp fire for a while chatting softly, listening to the night sounds of birds and animals. Sometimes there was a sort of rustling in the trees nearby.

'Possums out there,' one of them said sleepily.

Polly slept soundly until dawn pearled the dark sky's horizon. She lay quietly as the horses cropped the grass and as she sun rose the birds began their chirpy chorus only to be drowned by the laughter of the kookaburra — what locals called 'the settler's clock'.

Caroline Peterson was already raking up the embers of the fire to boil water for tea and they were soon on their way again now passing through thick forest to reach their next placement. A prosperous settler's wife had asked for a nursemaid and pronounced herself well pleased with the girl Caroline had selected, a girl from a large family in England who was well practised in childminding. The wife also had a nostalgic chat with Polly when she learned that Polly was from Castlebridge.

'Why, I'm from the next village, Featherstone. Some of my folks are still there.'

'And you've settled here well,' Polly

looked at the spacious house, with horses and paddock.'

'Indeed, I wouldn't go back to England for anything. I consider myself an Australian and my children of course will be Australian through and through. I love it here, I came on an immigrant ship twenty five years ago in terrible conditions, but I made it.'

'You're never homesick at all?' Polly was intrigued by the woman.

'I have to admit I was lucky, I married a good man who's done well, we have a great life.' She turned to Caroline, 'Now, Mrs Peterson, you shouldn't be sleeping out at night, next time you're passing we've ample room to put you all up.'

As they rode away from the house with their gradually diminishing band of girls, Caroline was well pleased with the visit.

'See, Polly, the personal meeting is a great asset to the business of providing places. News will get around, people will talk and I'll be able to place more girls in suitable loving houses.'

The next stop was a small town Caroline knew well through visiting an agricultural show. She had supporters and friends there who had set up a small depot where they could stay for a few days. A small temporary committee was set up to supervise feeding the party whilst three more of Mrs Peterson's protégés were placed with families.

Polly went along to see how the girls reacted to their new circumstances; some were shy to begin with but their new employers had been well vetted by Caroline and the girls could look forward to being part of family life. Polly noted Caroline's warm embrace as she left the girls in their new placements, bidding them to be good and industrious but making clear to both them and their new employers that if anything went wrong they could always return to their friend at Four Seasons.

The night of the trip was spent in a

busy town with several inns, at one of which, Caroline, Polly and the remaining protégé spent the night free. Another of Mrs Peterson's many benefactors being the owner's wife.

The last call was back on the road to Four Seasons. The lady of the house was another friend of Caroline's and was pleased to take the last girl on as nursemaid to her brood of young children. The shy young girl was pretty in a new grey dress with a white collar which Caroline had got to replace her faded sea crossing frock. Her fair hair was demurely parted and looped behind her ears, her blue eyes smiled as each child was introduced. She visibly relaxed as she saw the children were clean and well-mannered. Mrs Peterson and Polly said their farewells, Caroline promising to return to check all was well.

Once the carts were set for home Caroline spread her skirts on the seat and gave a contented sight of relief. 'Well, Polly, did you enjoy the trip?'

'I certainly did, it's an experience I wouldn't have missed for anything, so thank you, Caroline for allowing me to come.'

'You were an invaluable asset, and it was so good to have a female companion. Now, did you notice the young gentleman at the last house?'

'Just now? No.'

'Well as Amy was being introduced to her new charges he slipped away and came back a few minutes later, his face washed, hair brushed and a new kerchief round his neck. His eyes certainly lit up when he saw Amy.'

'Oh. Is that good?'

'Of course. I can see the whole happy picture, courtship, wedding, new home, children. If my work results in happy homes that's all I could wish for. Now it's time to get home to see what's been going on at Four Seasons.'

As the cart jogged homewards Caroline's eyes began to droop, her head nodded and she was soon fast asleep. Carefully Polly adjusted a rug around Caroline's knees and made sure her sun bonnet was securely tied. She was pleased to have a few moments of peace and quiet to gather her thoughts together. The trip had been a revelation, three nights and four days in which she'd met more people and seen more places than she'd ever experienced in Castlebridge.

Of course she missed her family, but this life in a new country was already binding her with ties she didn't want to break. The country was taking its hold on her, she wanted to see more of it, be part of it, do something useful for society like Caroline Peterson. How would even an office job in Fremantle compare to how she'd lived these last weeks at Four Seasons, and Billy — he was obviously in his element, how would school in a city far away from the freedom of the ranch suit her young brother?

He had been terrified by his young life in Castlebridge, how would he react to leaving Four Seasons? Too many questions, no answers. Polly gave up, turned her face to the sun after tying her own sun bonnet more firmly and gave herself up to the pleasures of the sights and sounds of a new country.

They stopped only once to rest and water the horses and around noon were close to the boundary of Four Seasons. Polly tried to suppress the feeling of coming home — Four Seasons was a temporary stopover, they would soon be moving on, pointless to become too attached to a place. They passed acres of young wheat before they reached the ranch house and paddock where the horses were kept. She sat up straight, shading her eyes from the sun, there were people in the paddock, riders and a familiar figure trotting confidently around the field.

'Why look, that's Billy surely?'

'Caroline looked up. 'I believe it is, he's about to take a jump — see, over that hurdle. Stop the cart, James, we'll watch him.'

'But Billy can't ride, he's never

ridden a horse before. He'll fall off.'

They were nearer now and Billy was preparing his horse to clear the hurdle, riding at some speed.

Polly clutched hold of Caroline. 'Oh my, what's he doing?'

'He's taking a jump, riding, we do a lot of that here, Polly.' She laughed. 'You had better get used to it, you'll be doing it yourself in no time. See, Billy's cleared the hurdle beautifully. Joe's in there with him, he's a great horseman, rides in shows, wins all the prizes, an ideal teacher for Billy.'

Billy saw them watching, waved and trotted his horse to the paddock rails. 'Did you see me?' He asked excitedly, 'Isn't it great, Polly? Jack says he'll let me have one of the horses for my own.'

'Billy, you did really well, I'm proud of you, but we can't stay here for ever. As soon as we hear from Uncle Harry we'll be off to Fremantle.'

The pleasure and excitement drained from his face. 'I don't want to go to Fremantle, can't we stay here?'

'Of course we can't, we're lucky to be here at all.'

'But Jack says I'm a . . . an asset to the ranch.'

'We don't want you to go,' Caroline Peterson chimed in, 'but you must do as Polly says, and you can always visit us whenever you like. Fremantle isn't that far away, especially now Jack's going to buy a motor vehicle.'

'It's not the same though.'

'Billy you've got to go to school,' Polly said firmly, 'so there's no more to be said.'

Caroline nodded to the driver and the cart began to move towards the house. 'It's a pity Billy can't stay here. Joe's done a good job teaching him to ride, he's a natural.'

Jack Makes A Discovery

As Polly followed Caroline Peterson into the ranch house it immediately felt like home, but because her family wasn't there it was followed by a twinge of guilt. Of course Castlebridge was home, but it seemed so far away and such a contrast to this new vibrant land, full of sunshine and so vast — she'd never be able to explore it all. For a second she closed her eyes imagining her father, Annie and her Donald, Uncle Harry and his family — all transported by magic to Four Seasons.

'Anything wrong, Polly,' Caroline asked.

'Oh no, sorry. I was . . . um . . . well, imagining my family from England here at Four Seasons. Just a silly dream.'

'Not at all, no reason why they shouldn't visit here. Plenty of room for everyone here at Four Seasons.'

'I can't imagine honestly that they would ever come.'

'Put your trust in the future, it's what I've always done.'

'I will try. Maybe one day . . . '

'Hello there,' Hannah and Mary, her sister, came running out to meet them, 'welcome back.' They hugged their mother, then Polly. 'Good trip? It's lovely to have you home. Did you really camp outdoors, Polly?'

'I did and it was wonderful. I enjoyed every minute.'

Caroline smiled. 'Polly was a great help and I'm trying to persuade her to stay longer at Four Seasons.'

'We'd like that too, and Billy loves it,' Hannah said, 'you should see him riding . . . '

'I have,' Polly looked worried, 'it's going to be difficult for him leaving here.'

'Well you know you are both very welcome to stay as long as you like.'

'I know. You've been so kind but it is impossible.'

'Well, let's enjoy the present, a welcome home supper will be on the table in five minutes. I hope you're all hungry.'

'Where's Jack?' Caroline asked.

'Out riding with Helen.'

'Will she be in for supper?'

'I don't think so, she's taking the horse home with her now she's used to it.'

'Is Jack going with her?'

'No, Joe is.'

'Joe?' Caroline frowned.

'What's wrong, Ma?'

'Shouldn't Jack be with her?'

Hannah shrugged. 'Not our business who she wants to go home with, she needs someone who's good with horses. Her new one's a lovely animal but a bit frisky. Joe's the best horse person we've got.'

'That won't please her father.'

'Well, they're all adults, Ma. We shouldn't interfere.'

'Hi there, travellers.' Jack appeared in the doorway, 'glad you're safely back.

Tell us about it, did you really camp out, Polly?'

'Course I did. Why does everyone think that's so strange?'

'No reason. Just living in England, I don't suppose there's much opportunity.'

'Certainly not where I come from, but there is some lovely countryside in the Yorkshire Dales — and lots of people go on camping holidays.'

'Sorry. Of course you have some lovely country areas. I'm glad you enjoyed the trip anyway. Billy will be along in a few minutes, he's just grooming the horse. Joe said you saw Billy on the way in.'

'We did. It was impressive.'

Hannah and Mary bustled into the room with hot dishes of food just as Billy himself came in. He nodded to Polly and muttered, 'Hope you had a nice time.'

'We did, thank you, Billy.' Her heart sank, the happy eagerness in his face when he was riding was gone, he was almost sulky. She hated to see him unhappy, maybe she could leave him at Four Seasons for a while anyway while she settled in Fremantle.

Jack had been carefully watching her throughout supper and as she started to help clear the dishes he put a hand on her arm. 'Polly, can we take tea out on the verandah?'

'I must help clear away . . . '

'No, it's all right, really,' Hannah said, 'there are enough of us here. Billy, will you help?'

'Sure, be glad to.' He still avoided looking at Polly.

'You are a lovely boy,' Hannah ruffled his hair, 'and I've some biscuits baked especially for you.'

'Sounds good to me,' Polly said, glad to see his usual smiling face again. 'Can't I help, I . . . ?'

'No.' Jack was sharp, 'I need to talk to you.'

'But . . . '

'Just trust me.' He turned to his sister. 'You don't mind?'

'Course not. I'll bring your tea out, although she might need something stronger.'

'Oh dear, what . . . ?'

Jack took her arm and led her outside to the wide verandah which ran round the house.

'What is it?' Polly asked in alarm as Jack sat down beside her on the swing seat.

'Polly, I don't quite know how to tell you this but . . . '

She jumped up, 'It's Dad, isn't it? Something happened to Annie?'

'No, no, they're all fine.'

'How do you know?'

'I've spoken to your Uncle Harry . . .'

'Uncle Harry . . . why . . . ? Tell me . . . '

'Sit down and calm down. Nothing's wrong at home except . . . your dad misses you and sister Annie is now officially engaged.'

'Good, I'm glad, but why . . . ?'

Jack took her hand and Polly didn't remove it. 'You see . . . ' he paused,

'Please Polly, don't look so frightened, it's sort of good news. You see I've found your brothers.'

For a few seconds the earth went spinning, Polly tried to get up but her legs felt weak and she collapsed back on to the seat.

'You've found my brothers? Where? How?'

'All in good time. I'll get the tea first and a glass of brandy. You've gone very pale.'

'Please tell me, I don't need tea now, just tell me . . . '

'They're both well, particularly Sam. Fred's a different story, but at least he's well.'

'Tell me, and where are they?'

'Not far from here.'

'What? Please . . . '

'They're in Fremantle right now.'

Polly was a stout-hearted and practical woman and had never fainted in her life, but as her head swam she leaned forward and would have fallen to the ground if Jack hadn't caught her.

He put his arm around her and held her close. 'Shush. It's all right. Ah Mary, good, tea. Thanks, and could you get a small glass of brandy. Polly's had quite a shock.'

'I'm all right now.' Polly drew deep breaths. 'Silly of me, but I was convinced in my own mind that my brothers were both dead. I just couldn't understand there was no word from either of them, and Uncle Harry too, he tried so hard. Oh, thank you, thank you, Jack. When can I see them?'

'As soon as you like, but it's not straightforward I'm afraid. Drink your tea while I tell you.'

Mary came almost running with a small glass of brandy. 'Is it bad news, Polly? From home?'

'Oh no, no, the best news I could possibly have. It's my brothers, and actually they're fine in Fremantle.'

Suddenly Polly put down her tea cup, flung her arms round Jack and kissed him.

He looked somewhat taken aback

then laughed, still holding her. 'My goodness, perhaps I can find some more family for you . . . '

'Oh sorry, sorry, I just couldn't . . . I'm so thankful. Thank you, Mary,' she took the glass, 'this'll perhaps calm me down. I must tell Billy and . . . '

'Of course, but let me tell you the story first. It's not all good news.'

'Oh, but . . . '

'Drink your brandy, try to relax, there are some problems.'

'What kind of problems? Are they ill? An accident at work? Have you seen them?'

'Yes, I have.'

'When can I . . . ?'

'Soon. Mary, could you just keep Billy occupied for a while, I want to explain things to Polly first.'

'All right, but don't be long. We all want to hear the good news.'

Left alone Jack took Polly's hand. 'Now this will come as a bit of a shock to you, both your brothers are in Fremantle but under very different conditions. Sam is older than Fred?'

'Yes. He always looked after Fred who's the fiery one, always in trouble, getting into fights. Sam's the steady one who used to bail him out.'

'That figures. I'm afraid Fred is in trouble again.'

'What? Here in Fremantle? I simply can't believe they're both here in Fremantle. How can I help? What can I do?'

'Just hear me out, Polly, then you can decide.'

'Sorry. I'll listen, I feel fine now, just grateful. How did you manage to find them so quickly?'

'Your Uncle Harry had done all the spadework already. The file you gave me threw up so many leads it was quite easy to follow some of them up from this country, much more difficult from England. I even knew one or two people at the mines they first worked in. I guess that's when they were writing home and sending money you said?'

'Yes,' Polly nodded, 'they were doing so well, then suddenly nothing after a place called Kalgoolie where they went first together.'

'They were making good money then, but they quarrelled, Fred met some men who wanted them to join in a venture further inland from Kalgoolie. It was a speculative venture, Sam refused to join in and tried to stop Fred . . . '

'I bet he went anyway, that'd be Fred, always wanted his own way.'

'It was a bad choice and got Fred into a lot of trouble. Sam heard rumours that conditions were bad where Fred had gone so he took time off to trek over to check. He'd heard rumours of a big fight and a robbery where the mine owner was killed.'

'Oh no, Fred wasn't involved?'

'He was, but he was trying to stop the riot and protect the mine owner. The mine workers had been drinking on a Saturday night, a fight started, the mine owner tried to stop it and got shot for his pains.'

'And Fred?' Polly asked fearfully.

'I'm afraid he was injured too. He stopped a blow to his head, a blow meant for the mine owner. Unfortunately there wasn't much medical assistance in the town nearest the mine and Fred was treated by a local doctor although he needed hospital treatment. Sam arrived a day or so later, took charge, arranged transport to take Fred to hospital and has been looking after him ever since.'

'That's terrible, Jack. Is he working?'

'Well there is some good in this story. Sam took a gamble, borrowed money, and bought up shares in the mine where they had started. It's still doing very well, your big brother, Sam, is a very astute businessman. He's grown quite wealthy these past months, he can afford the best treatment for Fred — that's why they're in Fremantle.'

'Is Fred . . . ?'

'Not too good, bad memory lapses, terrible headaches. When we talked he didn't make much sense, but Sam tells me he has made progress lately, some new medication.'

'Oh Jack, when can I see my brothers?'

'Just as soon as you like. Guess what, Sam has a motor car!'

'Wow! Really? This is all a dream, isn't it? I'm going to wake up in Castlebridge any moment now, and our Annie will be snoring beside me.'

'It's not a dream, it's real. You and I . . . we are real.'

They were very close, lips almost touching. Polly felt her heart beat faster, she wanted Jack to kiss her . . . but . . . she moved away quickly, she mustn't confuse sympathy with desire.

'So why didn't Sam write and tell us all this?'

'Sam will explain when he sees you. Oh, your uncle has telegraphed a money order to you, and details of the job he'd arranged for you in Fremantle.'

'Everything's happening so quickly, but I do want to see my brothers.'

'You'll tell Billy?'

'Of course, though Fremantle is like a red rag to a bull with him at the moment. He'll not remember much about his older brothers, there's twenty years between them and Billy went through a bad patch after they'd gone away. The whole family seemed to be disintegrating before Billy and I left.'

'So why did you leave?'

'Well, Billy . . . ' she stopped, 'Uncle Harry thought it would be good, a new experience, new country,' she improvised wildly, and knew by the look on Jack's face he didn't believe her. 'Thank you so much, Jack, for what you've done for me . . . for us.'

'A pleasure. So it was your uncle who did all the hard work, I'd like to meet him when I'm next in England.'

'You're going to England?' she had a picture of Jack and Helen on honeymoon in England. She banished it quickly, she'd had enough to worry about without pointless speculation about Jack and his Helen.

'Sometime in the future, after harvest maybe. Now let's go in and tell the others, they only know I found out where your brothers are.'

'I still can't believe it, and why on earth didn't Sam write and tell us. It was well over a year since we heard a word from them.'

'Don't blame Sam too much, he's had a hard time and he didn't want to worry you all. He just hoped things would settle down and it's only recently he's felt on top of the situation with Fred. You'll see anyway when we go in a couple of days.'

'Does my father know?'

'I believe your uncle Harry told him your brothers are alive and doing well, bit of a white lie, but probably kinder right now. Do you feel well enough to go in now?'

'Oh yes. I'm not ill, just . . . such a shock.'

Billy had already gone to bed by the time Polly and Jack joined the others and once Caroline and her daughters had heard the details of Jack's discovery it was quite late. The family kept early hours as farm work started at dawn.

* * *

The next day resumed as normal. Polly did the accounts from their trip and generally tidied up the paperwork. Caroline's net was spreading ever wide, there was correspondence, fund raising, planning the next trip to Fremantle Harbour to meet the next batch of female immigrants. Polly was glad to be busy but she couldn't help the whirling thoughts in her brain, and she wouldn't be happy until she'd actually seen her brothers for herself.

At the end of the day they all gathered for supper at Four Seasons and Jack told Polly he could take her to Fremantle the following day to see her brothers. 'Do you want us to take Billy?' he asked.

'I don't think so. He's avoiding me

just now, he wasn't at supper.'

'He took his food out to the stables, he's taking riding lessons from Joe.'

'It's going to be really hard for him to leave here.'

'I've told you he can stay, and now your brothers are in Fremantle . . . '

'He loves it here, Jack. I don't know what to do.'

'Nothing for the present. See how things are with Sam and Fred.'

'Probably best. Billy's just avoiding me lately, do you know he even slept in the stables last night.'

'But you'll tell him about his brothers?'

'Of course. When I've seen them.'

'Tomorrow.'

'I can never thank you enough, Jack, what you have done is incredible.'

'It's an incredible story and I'm just pleased to be part of it. Do you think your family in Castlebridge would come over to Fremantle . . . and your . . . er . . . boyfriend in England. Would he want to settle here?'

'What boy . . . er . . . well, I'm not sure . . . '

Jack frowned, then shrugged. 'We'll make an early start tomorrow, and I'm going to have a look at some motor vehicles. Sam is delighted with his car.'

'It's all so strange, to think of my brother with his very own motor car! He'd never have been able to have one in Castlebridge.'

* * *

Polly had little or no sleep that night, Billy's bed was empty so she presumed he was sleeping in the stables again, boycotting his sister and her plans to remove him to Fremantle. For a long time she lay awake thinking of her two older brothers so near to her.

It was almost two years since she'd seen them. She, Annie, and her father had waved them off at Castlebridge station to start their adventure. Little did she guess that she and Billy would be following them, fate reeling them all together thousands of miles away from home. She finally fell into a restless doze before she was awake again just before dawn.

Polly's Joy Is Tinged With Sadness

As Polly dressed in the pre-dawn light she tried to picture her older brothers but they refused to come into sharp focus. She had brought from home an old sepia photograph of the family group taken when she was a toddler.

In the picture she sat on her mother's knee, Billy was not yet born, Annie only just out of babyhood on the knee of a seated widow, Aunt Beatrice, long dead. Behind were the four Fletcher males: Uncle Harry, her father, George, smart in stiff wing collars and dark suits, and finally the brothers Sam and Fred, eager young faces ready to tackle the world.

Polly pressed the picture to her heart and made a wish that she would see the living ones together sometime in the future.

It was only just dawn but there was no sign of Billy. She went downstairs hoping to find him to tell him she was going to Fremantle and would see him at supper when she returned.

The house was very quiet as she went out on to the verandah, the air deliciously cool, the sky's dawn streaks already receding before the sunrise. It was going to be a very hot day, the men were probably out in the fields already catching a cool early start. She went down the steps, through the garden towards the paddocks where, to her astonishment, she saw a small knot of people including Billy who was grooming a horse. Standing by him were Joe, Jack, and a young girl — Helen!

Jack had his arm around her and was talking very earnestly to both Joe and Helen. Billy looked up from the horse, spotted Polly, then waved. The other three turned round and for a second or two no one moved, then Joe came across the paddock.

'Polly, you're up early. Billy's just

getting the horses ready for your trip into town.'

'Oh, Jack, you did say an early start?'

'Yes, sure. We'll go back to the house for tea if you like.'

Joe was already mounted. 'Thanks, Jack, I'll see Helen home.'

'Fine, but both of you think seriously about what I said.'

'I will, and have a good day in town.' They cantered out of the paddock to the track leading towards Helen's home ranch.

'I hope I haven't upset your plans,' Polly said. 'Didn't you want to go with Helen?'

Jack looked at her and frowned. 'Why? I'm not exactly her father's favourite person right now.'

'But . . .'

'It's complicated, I don't want to talk about it. I'm looking forward to the day in Fremantle; we'll see your brothers, then I've some business in Fremantle, actually it sort of concerns Helen. I've been putting it off, so seeing your brothers is a good excuse to get it over with, and then the best bit — I'm going to look at some motor vehicles.'

'A motor car?'

'Well, maybe. Not car right now, a motorised truck would be more useful to start with, it'll take at least half the time to town, so a quick cup of tea and we'll be on our way. All right?'

Polly nodded. 'I'm in your hands, Jack.'

He gave her a strange look, seemed about to say something then turned away and walked towards the house leaving a rather puzzled Polly to follow. There was something definitely in the air between Jack and Helen that she couldn't quite fathom.

* * *

The road to Fremantle was becoming familiar to Polly and she could recognise the different trees and animals. As they neared the town the air became oppressive and the heat heavy.

Polly was glad the horses were moving at a brisk pace creating a slight breeze on the open cart.

'Could be a last big summer heat wave, maybe a storm blowing up, another good reason to buy a motor vehicle. Not much fun in a storm in an open cart or on horseback. We're pretty much there now, your brothers are on this side of the outskirts of town.' He put a hand on her arm, 'You all right, not worried?'

'Well, no, once I've seen them . . . I just can't believe I am actually going to meet Sam and Fred, thousands of miles from home.'

'Well, they sure are looking forward to seeing you, though I must warn you Fred may take a little time to adjust.'

'Jack, I'm so lucky to have met you after our escape from Mimosa Ranch. Whatever would have happened to us?'

'I'm sure you would have thought of something, but it was a lucky day for me too. Ma would like you to stay on and help her with her immigrant girls.

Yes, I know you can't, your uncle, Billy's schooling — all of that, so you must do as you think best.'

He slowed the pace of the horses as they turned into a wide road with ranch style houses either side and plenty of space between. 'That's their house, the one with the verandah set back from the road, and I think, Polly, that's Sam in the rocking chair on the porch.'

'Is he expecting me?' Polly asked anxiously.

'I said I'd bring you as soon as possible so I guess he's on the look out now.' He halted the horses and helped Polly down from the high driver's seat. 'I won't stay long, just see you in, I'll be back in an hour or so.'

A tall dark-haired man came running down the wooden steps, a huge smile on his face. 'Polly! I can't believe it! My how you've grown.' He hugged her in a tight embrace and for a few seconds both were speechless.

Polly had to find a handkerchief to wipe away the tears before she could speak. 'Sam, I'm so happy to see you, I never dreamt it would happen in such a huge country and now I'm actually with my brothers.'

Sam said, 'This is just the beginning and Jack, we'll never be able to thank you for this because without you . . . '

'Nonsense, you'd have met up eventually in Fremantle. Your Uncle Harry was pretty near to solving the mystery of your whereabouts and Polly too would have tracked you down. Now I'm going to leave you, I've business in town which should take an hour or so. How's Fred?'

'Not too good, we'll have to take it slowly, anything that upsets his routine throws him right back into his shell. He's sleeping at the moment so we'll sit here, Polly, and catch up before I wake him.'

'Whatever you say, Sam. I'm just so happy to see you.'

'See you later then,' Jack said, 'see if I can't find a good motor deal.'

'Jack Peterson is a really good man,'

Sam said as they waved him off. 'You struck lucky there, and he's very keen on you.' He looked at her quizzically. 'Quite smitten by the way he talked about you when he came here before.'

'Oh, don't be silly, Sam, he's practically engaged to the daughter of his neighbour's farm.'

'That's a pity. Well, tell me all the news, why are you here? Jack didn't explain, just said that he found you and Billy in an old mining camp. I thought he was rambling, something about being on the run from a guy who wanted you to marry his son. It all sounds so unlikely, a far cry from Castlebridge.'

'It is. Sometimes I have to pinch myself to make sure it's not a dream, or a nightmare at one point.'

'My little sister,' Sam shook his head, 'and just Billy with you?'

'Yes. He's fine, loves working at Four Seasons, that's Jack's home.'

'Yes I know, but how . . . ?'

'I'll tell you later but now I want to

hear all about you and Fred. It all sounded dreadful, the fight . . . Jack told me.'

'Well, you know most of it then, Fred made an error of judgement, went with the bad chaps and he's paid the price. No, he's still paying for it now. You'll see shortly, but how's Dad, Annie, Uncle Harry . . . ' and so they talked filling in the gaps in their lives.

To Polly Sam seemed much older than his two years since he'd left England. He was still quite youthful in appearance, his hair still thick and glossy as she remembered it, but he'd added a beard which gave him an air of gravitas and experience.

'It was all so exciting at first, Polly, the mine did well, we made enough money to send home and . . .'

Polly broke in, 'Yes, that was wonderful but then suddenly no word, no letters or cards, nothing! As though you'd both vanished. Dad aged terribly, his health suffered and but for Uncle Harry I don't know what we'd have done. Surely you could have written to us, Sam. Dad was convinced you'd both died and it was worse after his accident with no work to go to and nothing to do but brood. He became more and more bitter, refused much of Uncle Harry's help, a whole year of fretting and worrying and our Billy going to rack and ruin, and no word from either of you.'

'Billy? But he's just a babby . . . '

'He's twelve, and he's had to grow up fast. We did our best but finally Dad washed his hands of him anyway,' she added, 'of course he's sort of fine now, but he missed his older brothers. Just letters would have at least kept the connection going.'

'Oh Polly, don't. I feel bad enough as it is. Please . . . ' he took her hand as the tears welled from her eyes, 'don't cry, we've found each other now. It'll be all right.'

'But why, Sam, why? Why no word?'

'Shush, shush, you'll wake Fred and I want you to be calm when you meet him. It may be a bit of a shock.'

'Oh no, is he really very ill?'

'He's over the worst so you're not to worry. I'll explain later. Dear Polly, the reason I didn't write was simply shame. We'd got into such a mess when everything was going so well because once I had to leave Kalgoolie to sort out Fred it was such a terrible situation. I just couldn't write about our troubles and I was ever optimistic things would get better as they did once I got Fred away, then I had to work so hard, day and night, to get on my feet again. Fred was in hospital for months . . . don't you see, Polly, how difficult it was?'

'Yes I do, but we're a family, Sam, and we could have helped.'

'But I'd let you down, and the irony is I was going to write this week. Fred's been out of hospital for quite a time, he's stabilising. I don't want a setback and I didn't want to burden you all with our problems when we were supposed to be making the family fortunes.'

'Jack says you are very wealthy.'

'Not very wealthy but at last money is not a problem, it's a good life out here and I aimed to fetch you all out to see for yourselves.'

'That's good, but we all wanted to know you were both still alive.'

'I'm sorry, it was selfish of me, but we must put it behind us now. I want to know why you came to Australia, surely not to look for us?'

'No . . . but . . . ' she was interrupted by a small movement behind her.

'Ah, it's Fred. He's woken up. Don't say anything yet, Polly, he needs time to adjust. Fred,' Sam called tentatively, 'out here.'

Polly held her breath but there was no sound or movement. 'What's the matter?' she asked.

'Ssh. He'll look through the window to see who's here, he's not happy with people yet.'

'Goodness,' Polly was alarmed, 'is he so bad, Sam?'

'It's unpredictable, he was good

when your Jack turned up so unexpectedly out of the blue, he took to Jack straight away.'

'As most people seem to,' Polly couldn't help saying.

'I'll go and fetch him.' Sam got up.

Alone on the porch Polly tried to stop the tears from starting up. Fred, her lively extrovert 'up for anything' older brother whom she idolised; always laughing, joking, full of plans for a bright future. She recalled one family Christmas just before their mother had died, Fred, the life and soul of the party, his first girlfriend, kissing her under the mistletoe to her embarrassment, Fred playing her along!

'Someone to see you,' Sam steered Fred out on to the porch but he tried to resist and go back into the house.'

'Not well enough today,' he muttered, 'tomorrow maybe.'

'No, now,' Sam steered his brother towards Polly, 'just sit down, Fred,' Sam said quietly, 'Polly and I are having a chat about old times. You might remember some of these too — in England? Castlebridge?'

Polly tried desperately to hide her shock, the dark-haired dashing young man she'd idolised had gone. This man looked more middle-aged, the dark hair was completely grey, he had a shuffling gait, shoulders stooped, eyes puzzled as he looked at her.

'Sit down, Fred,' Sam drew out a chair, 'sit down, just listen, you don't have to say anything.' To Polly he whispered, 'Just talk quietly about home, Castlebridge, Annie, Dad . . . '

Polly nodded. Fred's eyes began to focus as he looked at her. 'Well, Fred,' Polly tried to keep her voice steady, 'I'm here with Billy, our Annie, your little sister is engaged to be married to a lad called Donald Nightingale, they have a fine busy shop and café on the main street of Castlebridge. Do you remember it, Sam? Fred may too. Then there's Uncle Harry's little boy, he's nearly two so you won't have seen him. He's a lovely little child.'

'What's he called?' Sam queried.

'Wilfred. Aunt Victoria brought him to see us before we left England.'

'England . . . ?' suddenly Fred spoke, 'I remember, of course I do. It's where we live.' He looked around the room, a puzzled expression on his face, 'But . . . but this isn't the room we live in.' He looked at his brother, then at Polly and shook his head impatiently, ' . . . I don't understand, this isn't England, is it?'

'No, we're in Australia, we worked here then you had an accident, but you're getting better now. It's just that you're still a little confused about things. Don't worry, just relax, take it slowly.'

Fred smiled and suddenly Polly saw a glimpse of the old cheeky Fred. She smiled back, went over to him and put her arm round him looking to Sam to see if that was the right thing to do.

He nodded.

'Fred, I'm Polly, your sister. I lived in Castlebridge with our family, but I've come to Australia with your little brother, Billy . . . ’

Sam shook his head and mouthed, ‘too much — go slowly’.

Polly released Fred’s hand and went back to sit by Sam.

‘Billy?’ Fred frowned, ‘no — I don’t remember Billy,’ his eyes lit up, ‘but I do remember you, Polly, you’re my kid sister. You’ve grown and you’re very pretty. Are you married?’

‘No, I’m not married.’

‘Well I think you should be, haven’t these . . . er . . . Australian men any sense?’

‘Give her time, Fred, she’s only been in Australia a short while, that’s what Jack told us.’

‘Nearly three months,’ Polly said, ‘but it feels like for ever, so much has happened.’

‘We’d like to hear about it,’ Fred following Sam’s lead looked more alert and the awful blankness of his expression had disappeared.

‘Well, we left England . . . ’ and she told him about the voyage, their arrival with no-one to meet them, she told them about Mimosa Homestead but not about Bert's plans for marrying her off.

He began to look around. 'Polly?' he interrupted, 'I think I'll just lie down for a while. 'You won't go away, will you? I get tired you see.' He yawned. 'Have we had dinner yet, Sam?'

'Not yet. You have a little doze and we'll call you when it's dinner time.'

Fred got up and came over to Polly. 'Polly — yes from England. My sister!'

'Yes, that's right, Fred, but I'm here now, with you in Australia.'

'Is it Australia, Sam?'

'Yes it is, you go and have your rest and we'll call you at dinner time.'

'All right, Sam, but don't let my sister go, please. She's nice, isn't she?'

'Yes, and I won't. Come along,' he took his brother's arm and led him back into the house. He was gone for only a few minutes, not quite time enough for Polly to dry her eyes.

'Oh Polly, don't cry. He's made so

much progress. I'm happy for his future now. He'll never be the same man you and Dad saw off at Castlebridge a couple of years ago but on the other hand he's not the wreck I had to rescue a few weeks ago.'

'But he's ill, Sam. Mentally . . . '

'No. He's recovering well and there are new treatments all the time. Jack Peterson's given me the name of a doctor in Perth and there's a new clinic specialising in cases like Fred's. There's much to hope for.'

'I must help too. Is the clinic very expensive?'

'Enough, but you're not to worry about that. Wait until we hear from Uncle Harry.'

'But the money? How can you afford it — and this lovely house?'

'Didn't Jack explain?'

'Not in detail. You bought some mine shares.'

'Yep. I was, am, extremely lucky, I'd saved quite a bit when we first came out, I had the chance to invest in a new mine and it paid off. So, at the moment, I'm a comparatively wealthy man so you're not to worry about money. I'm happy to have that responsibility. I was hoping to send a tidy sum home to Dad but I'd best keep hold until I see how Fred gets on.'

Polly sighed, 'You don't know how good it feels to be with family again. I've so missed everyone, I didn't realise how much.'

'Uncle Harry has fixed a job for you?'

'Yes, I believe so. We are to pick up letters from the telegraph office. Jack will do that while he's in Fremantle.'

'So you'll probably be moving to Fremantle soon. I hope you'll live here, Polly, you and Billy.'

'Of course, if you'll have us for a while and if I can persuade Billy. He's completely besotted with Four Seasons.'

'He'll change his mind to be with family surely?'

'I wouldn't be . . . what on earth is that noise?'

'Sounds like a motor horn. Jack's left no time in keeping up with the times. Let's go and see what he's got.'

'What about Fred?'

'He'll come out if he's awake, he loves going for a ride in my motor car.'

'Amazing, you with a motor car. Whatever next? A leg up from Castlebridge dear brother.' Suddenly she felt full of hope for the future, and for the future of her family. It would tear at her heart to leave Four Seasons but it was impossible for her to be going on living there anyway when Jack married Helen. If only she could be sure Billy would settle happily in Fremantle.

As she went to see the magic motor Fred came out of his room. He took her arm as naturally as if they'd never been parted as they went outside.

Polly sent up a prayer of thankfulness for the happy moment, she knew from Sam that it wouldn't last but it was a good start. 'Goodness what . . . ? Is that a car, Jack?' She looked dubiously at the square metal box perched on four solid rubber tyres covered by quite ugly sort of mudguards.

'Splendid, isn't it?' Sam's face was alight with enthusiasm — he touched the metal bonnet with a sort of reverent awe. 'It's an Albion, isn't it?'

Jack nodded. 'Specially built for rural use, strong as a horse, top speed 15 to 20 miles an hour, open top so you get the open air, but you can roll the roof over in a rain storm.'

'Wonderful.' Jack and Sam couldn't keep their hands off it.

'I'll start her up, shall I?'

'Are we going back to Four Seasons in that?' Polly asked apprehensively. 'I thought you were going to buy a truck.'

'Ah well, changed my mind, unless you would like to drive the horse and trap back, Polly.'

'I could give it a try I suppose as it's the usual mode of transport — better get used to it.'

'No, only joking. I've to take this back to the motor sales shop, it's a shop model. If I like it, which I do, they'll order one for me. What do you think, Polly?' Jack asked.

'I don't know. I suppose it's progress of a sort but I do like the horse and cart. I'm sorry.'

'Aw, you'll get used to it. Bet you'll be driving one of these in a year or two,' Sam said, his head under the bonnet.

A Surprise Wedding Occurs

Polly followed Sam into the kitchen but he shooed her away. 'Go and talk to Jack, hasn't he got letters for you from your Uncle Harry?'

'They can wait, I'll help you with dinner.'

'No really, all done. I'm a dab hand at cold roasts and salads.'

'Truly? I don't remember you doing anything like that at Castlebridge.'

'Ah well, that was woman's work in Castlebridge. There weren't many women where I've been, at least not of the home-making variety.'

'Life's pretty different for you now.'

'Yep. I've had to be head cook and bottle-washer here, but it's luxury after some of the stuff we've had to live on in the mines. So you sit and enjoy the sun, read Uncle Harry's letters and keep Jack company.'

'All right, but give me a call if I can help.'

'All done. I've been planning this ever since Jack told us you'd be coming to see us.'

'I still can't believe it.'

'It is a miracle, Poll, and I'm so thankful we're all alive and sort of functioning.'

'You're doing wonderfully, brother Sam.'

She turned away to hide her emotion and sent a silent prayer of thanks to heaven before joining Jack on the verandah.

He handed her a package. 'Special mail delivery, must have cost your uncle quite a bit, apparently quite a batch: there's one from Annie, your Uncle Harry and a few others, and copies of references he's sent out to the office in Fremantle where he's arranged a job for you and information on a school where Billy has a provisional place.'

'Oh dear, Billy's not going to like that.'

'It's a good school in Fremantle, it's where Joe went and he loved it.'

'Will Billy settle in after living at Four Seasons?'

'Don't worry about that yet. Will you like moving here? I assume you'll stay with Sam and Fred.'

'Of course. It's wonderful how things are working out.'

'Aren't you going to read your letters?'

'Not just now. I'll wait until I'm home.'

'Home?'

'Er, sorry. Four Seasons I meant. It has been my home, Jack, these past weeks and it's been lovely, but I must move along.'

'But can't . . . ?'

'Grub's up.' Sam came on to the verandah staggering under the weight of an enormous over-laden tray.

'Goodness, how many's that for?' Polly asked.

'Just the four of us. I'll give Fred a call.'

Polly often remembered that meal at Sam's house with affection. The cold roast beef was the best she'd ever tasted, salads, bread, fruit and Australian pies bulked up the meal. Fred joined them and was entirely as Polly remembered her big brother from Castlebridge, until the end of the meal when he suddenly lost focus, stopped eating and whispered to Sam.

'Who are these two? I should know, shouldn't I . . . ?'

'Don't worry about it, you'll remember later. It's Polly, your sister and her friend, Jack.'

The puzzled frown cleared. 'Oh yes, I know but . . . Sam, I'm a bit tired, I'll lie down for a while.'

'That's perfectly all right, Fred. Don't forget to take your pills now.'

'I won't. Goodbye . . . um . . . all.'

Polly made to follow him but Jack stopped her. 'No, he's all right and he's done really well today. Your visit's done him good.'

'I hope so. I'll try to come again

whenever anyone on the ranch is coming to Fremantle. That was a lovely dinner and I'm very, very impressed.'

'Thanks, Sam,' Jack added, 'that was good and you must bring Fred out to Four Seasons sometimes if he'll come. Now, we should go, Polly, I'd like to get back before dark.'

'Sure.' Sam hugged Polly and shook Jack's hand. 'We'll see you again soon — in your new motor!'

Outside the horses were back in their shafts, no sign of the motor. 'The dealer picked it up while we had dinner, it's all arranged, he'll bring it down to Four Seasons when it's ready.'

'So I don't get to drive the cart then?'

'You'd like to?'

'I think I would. I need to get used to horses and it doesn't look too difficult.'

'Goodness,' Sam was astounded as she clambered into the driving seat, 'whatever next?'

'Change of roles, you cooked the meal, I get to learn to handle horses. All right, Jack?'

'Sure,' he smiled, 'nothing to it, and I'll be sitting right beside you.'

Sam watched them out of sight, gave a final wave and went inside to contemplate how their worlds had changed from their former lives in Castlebridge.

Polly was initially nervous as she took the reins, especially as one of the new motor cars came towards them on the road back to Four Seasons. The horses checked their steps and tossed their heads as the vehicle passed them.

'Keep a tight hold,' Jack guided her hands, 'don't let the horses know you might be bothered.'

'I won't, and I'm not — truly.' She clicked the reins like a professional and Jack sat back with folded arms.

'You're doing great, Polly, next thing you'll be riding one of the Four Seasons' horses. Let's get this ride done first.'

'We'll stop at the water hole to give the horses a break, I'll take over then, it'll be nearly dark when we reach Four Seasons.'

Polly was surprised she enjoyed driving the cart and was quite sorry when they reached the water hole.

'Well no problems, we can send you out any time with the horses, next step is to ride yourself, we've got plenty of horses. Nellie is a lovely docile mare, just right for a beginner.'

'But Jack, I won't be here long enough now it all seems set for Billy and me to settle in Fremantle.'

'Oh, I keep forgetting, you're so at home at Four Seasons that . . . ' He frowned. 'But Fremantle's not that far away.'

'We'll see. Goodness it's hot,' she rushed to change the subject, she didn't want to think about future problems.

'It's shady by those trees, I'll set the horses loose for a while,' Jack brought a rug from the cart and spread it on the ground, 'we won't stay long, I think there's a storm brewing up. We'll just about make it to Four Seasons before it breaks.' He lay back on the rug, hands behind his head, his eyes on Polly who sat demurely by his side. 'You do fit in so well at Four Seasons. It's a shame to move to Fremantle, town life, it's very different.'

'I know that, but I have to earn a living and now my brothers are there I can help out with Fred.'

'I suppose so,' he sat up and looked into her eyes, 'and your friend, the teacher in England, will he join you in Fremantle?'

'The teacher? Oh, Johnny you mean, actually there's a letter from him with Uncle Harry's. Er . . . no plans so far. I'll see how Billy settles in Fremantle and see what sort of job Uncle Harry's planned for me.'

'It'll be an office job?'

'I expect so, that's what I'm qualified for.'

'And you enjoy it?'

'Yes but . . . you see I've never done anything else before I came here, but I do like working with your mother.

Anyway, do you have any plans to visit England again?' She was anxious to turn the conversation away from herself.

Sitting in the warm sun, watching the water sparkling at their feet with Jack so close to her it would be too easy to fall even deeper in love with him. What she really needed was to be briskly practical.

He seemed in a dream too as he looked up at her, then he sat up straight and clasped his knees in his hands.

'England? I'd like to see my grandparents of course, but it's difficult at the moment. There are problems.'

'With the ranch?'

'No, well yes, in a way. You see Helen's father, Ken, is being very difficult, he's a strange man, a good farmer, he's done wonders with his land but he worries all the time about the future, he's a widower and he's desperate for sons . . . '

'Just like Bert Hackett — though he has a son of course.'

'Sons are important here, men who've worked hard to create a future . . .'

'Yes, of course,' she interrupted, 'but the women work hard too.'

'I know, but without children to carry on the line and consolidate the future all the pioneering work will have been for nothing.'

'Couldn't Helen's father marry again?'

'I suppose he could but he and Ruby, his wife, were so happy and she was the love of his life. He's been a changed man since she died and it's poor Helen who has to bear the burden of his anguish. He is just desperate for her to marry and produce a string of sons . . .' he stopped abruptly as a faint rumble of thunder sounded in the distance. 'Best move, Polly, the storm's a long way off, over towards Ox Bottom Creek, but Four Seasons would be in line of fire if it changes direction.'

'Wouldn't you all be glad of a rainstorm though for the crops?'

'Yes, but it's very dry and a lightning

strike could start a bush fire and we'd all be in trouble then. Let's get home quickly but,' he put his arm round her, 'it's been a good day, Polly. I really enjoyed meeting your brothers, you've got a great family. He bent to kiss her on the cheek but she turned her head in surprise and his lips touched hers. Fire shot through her as he kissed her and she lingered for a moment before drawing away.

Jack looked surprised then. 'Oh Polly, I forgot, you aren't free, I'm sorry.'

'But Jack . . . '

Too late, he was already hitching the horses into the shafts of the cart. There was another distant rumble and a far away brief vivid flash of lightning. He looked up. 'We'll be all right, it's moving away from the Four Seasons direction, but hold on, Polly, you'd best sit in the cart as I'm going to go as fast as the horses will go. It'll be a bumpy ride but we'll soon be home.'

It was quite a jolting ride but she managed to read her Uncle Harry's letters again to check the details. The 'nearly kiss' had convinced her she must leave Four Seasons as soon as practical. She had no excuse, no reason to stay at Four Seasons and her visit to Sam's had confirmed her future lay in the growing town of Fremantle.

The job her uncle suggested paid well and was a senior position in the business side of mining. It would be a challenge and would take her mind away from what was happening at the ranch house. As soon as they were back she would write and arrange to visit the offices of the mining company in Fremantle where she could call on Sarah Hackett's friend who she'd already written to give her news of Sarah and to explain what had happened since she'd left Mimosa Ranch.

In return she had had a cordial invitation to visit the friend at her home. Johnny Clark's letter had some surprises in it too. All in all Polly was a very lucky woman apart from inconveniently falling in love with Jack

Peterson! She would just have to get over that.

It was dusk when they arrived back at Four Seasons and the air was cooler. 'You all right, Polly? We're here, and the storm seems to have missed us. A pity really, it may have brought some rain.' He helped her down from the cart. 'Managed to read all your letters?'

'Yes. I'm surprised there were so many from family and friends.'

There was a pause.

'Your . . . um . . . teacher friend . . . did he write to you?'

'He did actually,' she said.

'Is he coming to see you?'

'Possibly. He's thinking of it.'

'Coming to Fremantle?'

'Well, yes, he is as soon as he can arrange a passage.'

'Well I think . . . '

But Polly never knew what Jack's thoughts were on the matter because a man came bursting out of Four Seasons. She recognised him as Helen's father, Ken Reynolds, who if anything was even more choleric than before.

Caroline Peterson was following, Hannah by her side. 'Do stop it, Ken, you'll do yourself some damage. There is no need to be so angry.'

'Of course there is, why can't Jack come right out with it and fix a date? It's not fair on Helen and it's not fair on me. I want some grandchildren, Caroline, surely you can't deny me that?'

'You can't simply buy yourself grandchildren, Ken.'

'Of course I don't want to buy grandchildren but it was all fixed years ago before your Archie died. Helen and Jack, they were kiddies, and aren't they fine specimens now? What the devil is your Jack playing at?' At that moment he saw Jack and Polly draw into the yard. 'Ah, thank goodness he's back. I'm going to get this straight once and for all so don't try to stop me.'

'Calm down, Ken,' Hannah said, 'we've some new arrivals from the boat, they'll be wondering what sort of place this is.'

'Let's get back inside then. Jack,' he bellowed across the yard, 'I need to speak to you right now and no more prevaricating. You've got to do the right thing by Helen.'

'Just let me stable the horses, they've had a long day, and I'll be with you in a few minutes. Go back into the house, Ma, you too, Hannah.'

'A good idea,' Caroline said thankfully. 'Polly, I'm dying to hear your news but there's a bit of a crisis here again and the new arrivals are in the dormitory. Here's a list of their names, they've only been here for a few hours, could you take some drinks and food to them, it's all laid out in the kitchen. Now, Ken please, come inside.'

'No, not until Jack gives me an actual date for the wedding, I'm not budging and that's that, I won't be sweet-talked any more. Name the date on which you'll marry my daughter or . . . '

'Or what, Ken?'

'I'll think of something you'll regret.'

'No point threatening, Ken, you'll just have to make the best of it.'

'What?' Ken stormed towards Jack who easily held him back at arm's length.

'Come on into the house, Ken. For the last time, all the hands are coming back from the fields, do you want them all to hear about your family business?'

'I don't care. The date, Jack?'

Polly was edging her way back to the house trying to be as inconspicuous as possible. She reached the front verandah steps when she heard Jack say, 'All right, Ken, if you want the world and his wife to hear about your domestic business, I'll tell you.'

The two men faced each other and a few of the farm hands nearby pretended to be forking straw and industriously sweeping the yard with their ears cocked for a battle.

'Polly,' Caroline called quickly, 'the girls are coming out of their building, probably frightened out of their wits, be a dear and show them into their rooms . . . er . . . tell them we're just settling an argument between friends.'

Polly nodded and moved away from the yard towards the new arrivals. 'Come on, girls, Mrs Peterson wants you all inside. It's supper time.'

'What's going on out there?' one young woman asked. 'Seems to be fighting talk, a bit scary, that older man, looks like he's fit to bust, do himself an injury if he's not careful.'

'It's all right, he's just a bit quick tempered, he'll calm down.'

'I like the look of the younger one,' a pretty young girl lingered behind, her eyes on Jack.

'He's the owner and he's spoken for.' Polly laughed. 'So don't get your hopes up. Here we are,' she did a quick head count as she shepherded them indoors. 'All present and correct, now let me tell you what happens next.'

Polly appeared calm and collected but her heart was thumping, surely there must be a showdown between

Jack and Helen's father. Jack must declare his commitment now. Through the window she could just see the corner of the yard, the two men facing each other. Jack was speaking but she couldn't hear what he said.

Out in the yard Caroline had persuaded the farm hands to go into the farm buildings but they could still hear the two men.

Jack was speaking calmly. 'Ken, I'm very sorry if we've misled you but I can never marry your daughter because . . . ' he took out his pocket watch, 'because now she is, I hope, already married, and I hate to say it but it's partly your own fault.'

The colour drained from Ken's face as he stared in disbelief at Jack.

'I'm sorry, but you were making life so difficult for Helen . . . '

'Who? I'll stop it. Where is she?'

'She's married to a good man and I think you know who it is — in your heart, and you must accept it.'

'It's . . . Joe, Joe Weston, isn't it?'

'It is. Helen and Joe have been in love for over a year and, but for your disapproval they would have been open about their love. I . . . '

With a cry of rage Ken launched himself at Jack, lashing out at him in fury. Jack easily fended him off as one of the farm hands came running out of the barn.

'Jack, do you need help? Mr Reynolds seems wild.'

'It's fine, Jim. Go back inside please.'

'Joe Weston,' Ken's fury was draining away, his arms hung limp by his side, his face anguished. 'It was all planned out, you and she — and the two farms, a fine spread of land, thousands of acres, there'd be children to carry on — a dynasty.' He looked blankly at Jack. 'Is it too late to stop it?'

'They are married, early this morning. They'll be away for a day or two.'

'Where are they?'

'I'm not telling you just yet . . . '

'But Joe Weston . . . why, he's a nobody, with nothing. We're ruined.'

'Don't be silly, Ken, Joe Weston is far from being a nobody and he'll make Helen a fine husband.'

'But . . . you and she . . . Helen said . . . '

'I know and maybe it was wrong of us but we had to sort things out, put you off the track for a while.'

'Jack.' Caroline and Hannah came towards them, 'what on earth is going on? Ken, you look terrible. What's the matter?'

'Helen — she's . . . she's married.'

'Married? How? Who?'

'Ask your son. Seems it's been planned all along — behind my back. Married to Joe Weston — a hired hand.'

'To Joe?' Caroline gasped, 'but that's not possible, she's engaged to Jack.'

'No, Mother, we were never engaged. You all just hoped we were.'

'And it appears my daughter is married to a mere farm hand.'

'Joe's a lovely man,' Hannah frowned, 'even if he is only a farm hand. Don't be such a snob.'

'Joe is much more than a farm hand,' Jack said, 'and I suggest we all go into the house, have a drink, calm down, and I'll set the record straight.

'But . . . ' Ken started to protest but Caroline and Hannah took an arm each and gently led him into the house.

Billy Causes A Panic

Caroline Peterson steered her neighbour towards a small room at the back of the ranch house, Jack followed with his two sisters, then Caroline released her neighbour.

'Now Ken, sit down in this chair and don't say a word until your breathing is easy and your heart rate's dropped. Hannah dear, there's some home-made sloe gin cordial in the dining room, could you bring it in with some glasses? It'd be a restorative all round.'

'I'll help,' Mary followed Hannah out of the room.

Ken Reynolds was silent, eyes fixed on Jack, now puzzled more than angry. 'So, Jack, what's this all about? You're not going to marry my daughter obviously and you've never been in love with her?'

'Ken, Helen is a good long-standing

friend, but I've never loved her and she's never loved me except as a friend.'

'So where are they now, and are they really married? Was it an elopement? Why, Jack, why? Caroline, were you in on this elopement?'

'Of course not. I was as anxious for Jack to marry Helen as you were, it's a shock to me too but don't worry, Ken, and I'll explain why shortly.' She turned to her son. 'Jack, I do wish you'd confided in me, it would have saved all the heartache and anger.'

'I don't see how, Helen was frightened of you, Ken, you were so desperate for us to marry just to amalgamate the two ranches.'

'Nothing wrong with that,' Ken said gruffly.

'Not if it means a marriage of convenience.'

'But you acted like you were in love,' he shook his head in bewilderment, 'couldn't she have talked to me . . . ?'

'No, Ken, I'm sorry, but your daughter was frightened of you, you've a fiery temper when you don't get your own way and she was frightened for Joe too.'

'Frightened? Of me? I wouldn't hurt a single hair of her head, she's precious to me . . . '

'You were prepared to commit violence on Joe just now, that's why they had to meet secretly and why I agreed to act as decoy for a while.'

Hannah and Mary came in with a laden tray. 'Sloe gin, bread and cheese, to keep us going, calm our nerves. Hope we haven't missed anything.'

'No.' Jack went to pour the sloe gin and Hannah handed round the bread and cheese. 'Now, let's all relax, what's done is done, and I don't regret my part in it. Sorry, Ken, but I know Helen and Joe will be very happy. Where's Polly by the way?'

'Looking after the new girls. Polly's not family, Jack, it won't mean anything to her.'

'I guess not. Fair enough,' but in his heart he wished she could be there — a steadying presence. 'Ken, you feel calmer now?'

'Yes, but I can't believe what you just said . . . frightened of her dad? That's terrible. I just didn't want her to marry a . . . a nobody. Joe Weston's just a hired hand . . . '

'Stop that, Ken,' Caroline spoke sharply, 'you know nothing about Joe Weston.'

'A hired hand,' Ken repeated, 'he's got nothing to bring to Helen.'

'I said stop!' Caroline raised her voice. 'Listen to me, you too, Jack, I blame you for not telling me about this . . . this charade at being in love with Helen. All this could have been avoided.'

'All right, maybe I should have talked to you, but Helen was so worried and frightened that Ken would do something to Joe.'

'I think you're wrong, but never mind it's all in the open now, except none of you know the whole story.'

Caroline looked round the room, the

walls covered in maps of many countries, countries where Caroline and her family had lived, following her husband's military career. She touched a map of India with a nostalgic smile. 'We were so happy in India, Archie and me, that's why I've brought you to this room. It was Archie's favourite place where he could look back over his wonderful career as a soldier. You didn't really know my husband did you, Ken?'

'I met him after he retired from the army, when he came to join you, Jack and the girls, but no, I didn't really know him. He died not long after he retired, didn't he?'

'Yes. He loved army life but he was full of plans for Four Seasons once he'd retired. When Jack left his grandparents in London Archie and Jack worked the farm together. He was very happy with Jack and Joe until he died.'

'Ma, I'm sorry, but what's this to do with Joe and Helen?' Mary asked.

'You'll see, I'm just calling up Archie's presence in a way. You see,

Ken, it was Archie who found Joe and that eventually brought Joe to Four Seasons to work on the ranch.'

There was silence for a few seconds until Ken said, 'So, your late husband, Archie, found himself a hired hand and a good worker I admit, but I still don't see what that has to do with sloping off with my daughter — probably hoping to benefit from my land too . . . '

'Just stop it, Ken.' Caroline was angry, 'why do you always look on the black side . . . ?'

'Because that's what it's been! Ever since my Ruby died.'

'I'm sorry, but that was six years ago. Now it's time to move on.'

'That's why I wanted Helen to marry Jack, amalgamate the two farms for the next generation.'

'Well it's time to stop being so selfish and look beyond what you want.'

'It's all gone to pot any case, I might as well sell up and have and easy life, go and live in a town — Fremantle, even Sydney. Miles away.'

'Oh do stop pitying yourself,' Caroline groaned, 'just let me tell you and don't interrupt.' Caroline took a deep breath. 'First, Joe is a good, splendid man, you are lucky to have such a man marrying your only daughter.'

'But . . . '

'Shush, not a word,' Hannah had her finger to her lips.

Caroline ignored the interruptions. 'Joe Weston has all the attributes needed for marrying Helen — he is not simply a hired hand, he's a Peterson too, with Peterson blood in his veins — from his mother's side, so he is in effect a member of our family.'

'A Peterson,' Ken couldn't be silent. 'It's not possible, he's Joe Weston, always has been as long as I've known him.

'Weston was on his name tag at the orphanage where Archie found him.'

'Dad found him!' Jack exclaimed.

'Wow,' Hannah said, 'what's his story then?'

'And why?' Mary added.

Caroline sipped her drink. 'I can tell you, Joe's father was a young soldier under Archie's command. Before a major battle the soldier came to Archie to tell him he'd fallen in love with a young immigrant girl from England who was working as a house servant in India. She was pregnant by this young soldier, Joe's father, and he had a premonition he wouldn't survive the battle. He asked Archie to take care of things if he was killed. He was worried because the girl had threatened to kill herself and the baby if the soldier was killed.'

'Oh no,' tender-hearted Mary gasped.

'Exactly, so when the soldier died Archie went to the hospital. The girl had had her baby, but sadly the mother had died in childbirth. Joe Weston, born thirty years ago in India to Herbert Weston and Dora Peterson.

There was silence, then he muttered, 'Even so, but well frankly he's born out of wedlock and he's penniless.'

'Ken, show some charity,' Caroline

spoke severely, 'judge a man by what he is, a good person, we all know him, and Joe isn't penniless, his mother was a Peterson, admittedly not wealthy but her family in the north of England weren't poor — but they had a large family. Dora was eventually sent to be a governess in India to better herself.'

'So why hasn't Joe Weston admitted all this?' Ken asked.

'Because Joe Weston is a very proud man, and because he is intensely loyal to the grandparents who brought him up. Archie traced the soldier's family and took the baby to England himself. He found Joe's paternal grandparents who, though elderly, were delighted to rear baby Joe. Archie helped financially but when the grandparents died we lost touch with Joe until he turned up here as a young man looking for Archie. We took him in and he's been with us ever since — part and parcel of our lives.'

There was a long pause, Jack topped up the glasses.

'But . . . ' Ken frowned, 'why did he have to keep it such a secret?'

'I've told you, Joe's a very proud man, he has a chip on his shoulder about his background, in fact he refutes the Peterson part of himself. He was very fond of his grandparents, especially as they'd lost their only son, his dead father's a Weston through and through, but there is definitely Peterson blood in his veins. Had I known it was Joe Helen was in love with I would have told you straight away.'

'I wish you'd told me anyway,' Jack said, 'because when I went to Fremantle I saw a lawyer about taking Joe into partnership. I've set the wheels in motion and Joe will have an equal share in the running of Four Seasons, I've thought a lot about it for a long time now.'

'Really?' Caroline raised her glass. 'That is wonderful, and I can also tell you all that Archie left money in trust to Joe. He hasn't touched a penny yet but if the partnership goes ahead I'm sure he'll put that money to good use on the ranch.'

'Satisfied, Ken?' Jack asked.

'It's a lot to take on. I'll wait until they both come back from wherever they are.'

* * *

Back in the immigrants' dormitory Polly was listening to the tales of the newly arrived immigrants. She'd been across to the house to collect the girls' suppers and had been aware of the buzz of conversation from along the corridor. Now she was settling the girls in their beds and taking details of their histories when Geoff, one of Jack's numerous cousins working at Four Seasons burst in.

'Polly? There you are. Hi girls, sorry to barge in at bedtime but I've been listening to the wireless. There are bush fires coming this way, there were lightning strikes, they're a long way off heading towards Fremantle but we have to take all the usual precautions.'

'Fremantle?' Polly's first thoughts were for Sam and Fred.

'Oh, far away from the town, safe there, but there's a stretch of bush between here and Fremantle. I need to warn everyone. Where on earth is everyone, Polly? I've been to the house but no-one's about.'

'I think they're all in the back, shouldn't we go over . . . ?'

'Sure can. Can you leave the ladies?'

'I think so. You'll all be all right, girls.'

They nodded, it had been a long day and most of them were already nodding off.

Polly and Geoff walked towards the house. 'Is it really dangerous?' Polly had read about Australian bush fires and didn't like what she'd read.

'We'll be fine, and the fire fighters are already out, but it's as well to be prepared. I see there's a new batch of Aunt Caroline's immigrants.'

'Yes. Only arrived today.'

'She does a wonderful job, doesn't she?'

'Yes, she's very committed.'

'Ah, looks like the meeting, or whatever it was, is over.'

'Geoff, Polly,' Caroline came down the front steps, 'anything wrong? The girls?'

'All tucked up. We came to tell you about the fires, heard on the wireless, between here and Fremantle, lightning strikes, it's under control but there is a high wind forecast and we've had little or no rain for weeks. The ground's tinder dry. I reckon we should keep an eye on things during the night.'

'Thanks, Geoff,' Jack joined him, 'I'll give you a hand.'

Now everyone was crowding round, asking him questions.

'Don't panic,' Jack called out, 'we're quite safe here but we always have to take precautions. Polly, are the ladies all right?'

'Yes, all tucked up in bed.'

'Good, we won't need to worry about

them. Ma, are you going in to say goodnight to them?'

'I certainly am. I'll stay there too, I've a camp bed there. I usually sleep there the first night or so — so you will let me know if there's any change?'

'Do you want me to stay?' Polly asked.

Before Caroline could reply Ken was shouting out, 'Jack, where are Helen and Joe? They may be in the line of fire.'

'No, no,' he shook his head, 'they're in Perth by now so no worries.'

'Hmm, I'll have to think about that. Maybe I have been living in the past, you see ever since Ruby died I . . . '

'I know, Ken, but you've lots to look forward to, and I say again, Joe Weston is a very good man and Helen's a lucky girl. They will be very happy and give you lots of sons, maybe even a girl or two, think of that, Ken. But let's deal with this fire first.'

'Right. Give me a job to do.'

'Well, if you check off all the men who stay on site first, and maybe keep your ears open for more news on the wireless.'

Jack took charge of the operation 'fire alert', checking on the animals, horses first. He sent a couple of men out to check the sheep, thinking that they may have to be brought nearer the homestead. He shuddered at the thought of the fairly recent neighbouring fire further east at the Prickly Bear Estate where 600 acres of grass were burnt and 100 sheep roasted.

Polly and Caroline checked the new immigrants again, a few were asleep but several were chatting, trying to ward off home-sickness.

'You can go now, Polly, if you want, I'll stay here all night.'

'Oh, I'll come back but I haven't seen Billy at all — and his bed's not been slept in again. I'll go and find him, he's probably helping Jack.'

Outside oil lamps lit the scene as men checked hoses, water tanks and fire fighting equipment. The yard was full of activity.

'Polly,' Jack called out, 'everything all right with the girls?'

'Yes, your ma's with them, some are a bit scared, worrying about the fire.'

'Tell them there's really nothing to worry about, for them anyway. The wind direction is moving the fire away from us, back towards Fremantle, but we always have to assume the worst and be ready for it, it . . . '

'Jack, Jack, quick, over here,' one of the men came running into the yard waving an envelope.

'What's the problem, Geoff?'

Geoff glanced at Polly then back to Jack with a worried frown. 'Er, I'm checking the horses — all in bar one, the new roan, the one . . . er . . . ' he glanced at Polly, 'young Billy was riding.'

'What?' Polly said, anxiety clutching at her breath.

'Billy. I haven't seen him, have you, Jack? He hasn't slept in his bed for days.'

'No, he sleeps in the stables, above

the loft. Geoff, you're sure you haven't seen him?'

'No, I've asked around, no-one's seen him but there's a note, by Nero's stall, addressed to you Polly. Here.'

Fingers fumbling to open the folded paper Polly's throat went dry, she took in the brief contents at a glance and pressed her hand to her heart. 'Jack, Billy, he's gone, taken Nero . . .' trembling, she handed Jack the paper.

He read it out: '*Polly, I'm not going to Fremantle or to school. I'm going to find a ranch where they'll have me to work. Please don't try to follow me, don't worry anymore about me, you have done enough. Say sorry to Jack, Joe, and all the men. Thank you, Four Seasons. Billy.*'

Polly's cry of anguish rang through the yard. She turned to Jack who took her in his arms.

'Shush, shush, you mustn't worry. We'll find him.'

'But the fire, he's heading straight for it.'

'We don't know that. Geoff, do we know how long he's been gone?'

'I haven't seen him all day. Maybe someone has.'

'I must go after him,' Polly cried out, 'he won't even know about the fire. He'll be caught, he doesn't know how, he . . . '

'Stop it, Polly,' Jack still held her, 'we'll find him. Let me quickly check with the men.'

'I'll help,' Geoff said.

'Don't just leave me here, I've got to come with you, please!'

'All right, but it'll mean riding up behind me. Could you do that?'

'Of course I can, anything. Oh Billy, Billy . . . '

'Polly,' Jack released her and gave her a little shake, 'if you want to come you'll have to . . . '

'I know, I know, I will keep calm,' she drew a deep breath.

'Geoff, can you and the others manage here?'

'Sure we can. Will you want any help

looking for Billy?'

'It'd help, yes. Can you arrange that? Polly, come into the house, you need some breeches, Hannah's about your size, we'll kit you out then leave straight away. Ask around, Geoff, and meet us here in ten minutes.'

'Yep, I'll come with you myself if you like.'

'Thanks, that'd be a help. Saddle up the horses when you've done the rounds.'

'Will do.'

Jack took Polly's arm as they walked quickly towards the house.

'Billy, oh Billy,' Polly sobbed quietly.

Jack stopped. 'Polly, I said . . . '

'Yes, yes, sorry. I'm . . . um . . . fine, you'll see.'

Jack gave her a little shake, then held her tightly in his arms. 'Of course you are, stay strong, and I promise you we will find Billy.'

But Polly couldn't erase the image of her little brother surrounded by flames with no escape — and it was all her fault.

'No-one's Seen Billy'

Caroline Peterson came into Hannah's room where Polly was pulling on riding breeches and boots. 'What on earth is going on?' Caroline frowned, 'the ladies are all tucked up but there's such a commotion outside one or two were frightened. The fire's not coming this way. We're safe.'

'Yes, for now. It's not the fire . . .' Hannah started to say . . .

'It's Billy.' Polly was struggling with the boots, 'I've got to find him, he's run away . . .'

'Run away, but why?'

'Because he doesn't want to go to Fremantle at any price. I should have taken more notice.'

'Polly, it's not your fault. We'll find him, and he can work here, he knows that, but you can't hold the men up. Jack's going I assume, and Geoff, he found Billy's note. Billy's taken the horse, Nero, the one he's been riding. Polly, you can't go,' Caroline repeated firmly.

'I must, I can't simply wait here, I'd go mad.'

Caroline sighed. 'All right but it won't be easy. You've never ridden a horse, but I'll come and you can ride behind me. You're no weight at all . . . '

'But the ladies?' Polly asked.

'I'll see to them,' Hannah said, 'I think Polly should go, it'd be awful here worrying and fretting.'

'When was Billy last seen?'

'I'm not sure,' Polly replied, 'Geoff's asking around now.'

'So — I'll quickly pack the thermos and . . . '

'No, no, we have to go now,' Polly cried.

'By the time the horses are saddled up I'll be outside with some food. You've had a long day, Polly.'

'Now, we need to go . . . ' Polly was nearly weeping.

'Polly,' Jack spoke sharply, 'you promised.'

'All right,' she took a deep breath. 'Yes, sorry . . . I'm calm. I won't interfere, but can we see if Geoff's got any information about Billy?'

Once in the yard they saw a huddle of workers round Geoff. 'Jack, all the men are here but no-one's seen Billy since early morning. He was up before dawn, saw to the animals, then told Jim here he was getting something to eat. That's all we know.'

'How did he seem?' Polly asked, 'was he upset at all?'

'No, his normal cheerful whistling self. Jack, do you want anyone else on the search party?'

'Oh, please, yes,' Polly cried.

'No, Jim, but thanks,' Jack said firmly, 'Geoff's coming and so is my mother. We need people back here in case the fire changes direction and we have to evacuate. Billy may come back here, and there's Ma's ladies too.'

'What route are you taking?' Jim asked.

'We'll head east in a northerly direction, there's a fire station lookout quite near, they'll have all the latest news.'

'Here we are, Polly,' Caroline and Hannah came into the yard, 'horses ready?'

'Ready and waiting.' The men clustered round the horses as Jack swung up into the saddle.

'Polly, sure about this? You too, Ma?'

'We'll be fine,' Caroline saddled up, 'Now, Polly, foot in the stirrup, someone give her a push up, swing yourself over, good, well done, hold on tight and we're off. You'll soon get used to the motion.'

Polly closed her eyes and hoped for the best. For a time she felt dreadful but her little bit of driving the cart earlier helped her confidence, though she still clung tightly to Caroline as the encouraging farewells from Four Seasons faded away.

The motion of the horses, the strangeness of the situation distracted her a little from worrying about Billy. It was still just light when they reached the first fire lookout, a cabin-shaped box perched on very high stilts to give a long range view over the treetops.

Jack called a halt as a man came out on to a railed platform. 'Hi folks, where're you heading? I wouldn't advise any travel this way at the moment.'

'We're looking for a boy, missing from Four Seasons, boy about twelve on horseback. Has he passed by this way?'

'Seen no-one all day. God help him if he goes in the wrong direction.' The fire scout looked down on them through binoculars. 'Couple of women there with you?'

'My mother and the boy's sister. We're very worried about him, he won't have heard about the fire,' Jack said.

'I'll telegraph around to the other lookouts, Mr Peterson. How long's he been lost?'

'Less than a day, left Four Seasons

early this morning.

'Do you know where he's heading?'

'No idea, that's the trouble.'

'Towards Fremantle? Looking for a ship maybe?'

'No. Ranch work is what he wants.'

'Well that kinda narrows it. Bella Vista spread is north, and that's where the fire's heading. Oxbow River's west, maybe take a swing that way, his best bet most likely though is Mimosa, Bert Hackett's place, not far out of Fremantle, it's out of reach of the fire unless there's an unlikely change of wind speed. I would . . . '

Polly interrupted him, 'Mimosa — of course! Jack, that's where he's gone it's obvious, he liked it there, loved the animals, even Bert had nothing but praise for him. Billy didn't want to leave. Ask the man, Jack, if the fire's near Mimosa.'

'I hear you, Miss, I can't tell you for sure but it's your safest bet I'd say, and there's a river on that property, might be useful.'

'Jack, what'll we do?'

'You could well be right, Billy talked a lot about Mimosa and he's too bright a lad to set off on his own without a plan. If we do go that way and we reach the Aborigine trail we'd be past the worst of the open scrubland and bush.'

'Could be a needle in a haystack if we don't plump for Mimosa,' Geoff said.

'Tell you what . . . ' the look-out man had climbed down to the ground, 'you folks have a real dilemma. Reports coming in say it's unpredictable because of the changing weather conditions, yesterday it stormed through sparsely populated bushlands up north, but it's picking up terrific speeds, nearly sixty miles an hour. If that northerly direction holds, you folks are safe to hit Mimosa and your brother, Miss, will be safe too.' He shrugged, 'The other way, as the man said, 'needle in a haystack'. Frankly, to be brutal, sorry, Miss, you could all be burnt to cinders.'

Polly tried to stifle a cry.

'Sorry,' the man repeated, 'but with ladies in the party, maybe turn back, see what fits.'

'Young man,' Caroline said sternly, 'I've lived here many years and been in many situations more dangerous than this, so we'll go the way most likely to find our boy. Mimosa — all agreed?'

'Sorry, Ma'am, no offence.'

'None taken. You've been very helpful.'

'Billy's got too much commonsense not to have had a plan,' Polly said.

'So Mimosa it is,' said Jack.

'It's your only safe bet,' the man said, 'you just have to hope your hunch is right, Miss. I'll keep looking and I'll pass the word along to all the other lookouts. Best of luck.'

Dusk was falling rapidly, the wind speed increasing but still blowing north, away from Mimosa Ranch. Polly, forgetting the numb pain from so many unaccustomed hours in the saddle prayed for Billy's safety as well as their own. Quite suddenly dusk turned to dark and a very faint orange glow outlined the far horizon.

'Don't worry, Polly,' Caroline sensed her unease, 'honestly the fire's miles away. See, the sky is totally dark where we're heading.'

They stopped briefly to rest the horses and drink from a thermos of coffee.

'How many miles from Mimosa?' Polly asked.

'The miners' camp where we found you and Billy is about an hour away, then almost there. You and Billy walked there from Mimosa, didn't you?'

'It didn't seem far, we were intent on running away. Ironical isn't it if Billy is really making for there?'

'We have to hope he is,' Caroline said soberly. 'Wind speeds are picking up, pray it doesn't change.'

'We'd have to stop over at Mimosa anyway,' Geoff said, 'the horses won't last without a rest past there.'

No-one spoke, if Billy wasn't at Mimosa he'd be lost in the bush by now unaware that the fire could be approaching from any angle. Polly didn't dare think beyond getting to Mimosa. As they neared the mining camp the glow to the north grew brighter and Polly suddenly coughed. 'Smoke,' she gasped, 'it's near.'

'No, miles away. Truly,' Caroline said, 'there's no town between it and the fire, nothing to absorb the smoke. If it gets worse we'll stop and tie damp clothes over our mouths.'

'No, no, we're nearly at the camp. It's not far.'

Suddenly Caroline's horse reared up in fright as a truck with lights blazing came travelling at speed in the middle of the track.

'Hold tight,' yelled Caroline as Polly felt herself sliding away from the saddle. She hung on by her fingertips to Caroline's saddle as the horse was brought under control.

Geoff reined their horses to the side. 'What on earth?'

The truck had stopped and was now

reversing rapidly towards them. Jack and Geoff dismounted quickly and ran to the car.

'You what?' Geoff shouted. 'Where? Jack, it's Bert Hackett — from Mimosa.'

'Jack Peterson, and you, Geoff. Haven't seen you in a long time.'

'Nor me you. What are you doing here?'

'Mission of mercy!' Bert climbed out of his truck. 'Hello, Mrs Peterson — good God, is that Polly Fletcher — on a horse?'

'Bert, please, have you seen my Billy? He ran away this morning and he didn't know about the fire.'

'Yes, it's pretty bad, but I think we're safe so far so long as the wind . . .'

'Bert . . . Mr Hackett . . . please . . .'

'Course we've got young Billy. Where else would he have gone but where he was happy. Turned up dead-beat an hour or so ago, fed and watered him and he's out for the count — fast asleep.'

'Oh Bert,' Polly's tears flowed freely.

'Thank you, thank you . . . '

'I should think so, running off like that, hurt me very much after all I'd done, and taking Billy away from where he was so happy.'

'All right, Bert,' Jack said, 'we're very thankful, and thankful too that the fire isn't coming our way.'

'Not yet it isn't — but Mimosa's not really in danger — too near Fremantle.'

'So when can I see Billy? Please, Mr Hackett.'

'Where are you off to, Bert, in such a tearing hurry?' Jack was curious.

'To tell you the lad was safe of course. He was really worried sick about you, Polly, especially when he heard about the fires — regretted running off I reckon.'

'Mr Hackett, thank you, I can never thank you enough . . . '

'Well, you did a lot for my Sarah. She worried about you, she was delighted to see Billy. I think, since you came, Polly, she's in better health.'

'I'm so pleased. I'd love to see her.'

'I suppose you lot expect me to put you up for the night. Good job I bumped into you.'

'Almost did,' muttered Geoff.

'I'm just thankful to all of you, and I'm sorry we ran away, Mr Hackett, but it wasn't right to try and make me marry Colin.'

'Not a problem. You see, our Colin has finally found a wife. Picked her himself at Fremantle. Lovely woman, from London, a bit older than Colin, sensible sort, looks after the boy a treat. Gets on well with Sarah, too. Wedding's next month, so a happy ending all round.'

'Looks like it. I'm so glad, Polly,' Jack moved towards her and put an arm round her shoulders, 'you did well on the horse but you'll be stiff and sore in the morning. You'll probably need some embrocation.'

As she looked up at Jack, Polly longed for the love and comfort to be held closely in his arms and share her profound relief they were all out of danger. Jack Peterson would always be her first and only love, but she quickly moved away from him. She had everything to be thankful for, Billy was safe and that was all that mattered. She would move to Fremantle but leave Billy at Four Seasons, however painful it would be to see Jack and Helen as man and wife, whenever she visited Billy, as she was still unaware of Helen and Joe's marriage.

She was glad to ride to Mimosa in Bert's truck. She was already stiffening up but was now determined to learn to ride as soon as possible in the future.

As they approached Mimosa Bert said gruffly, 'Sorry you felt you had to run away so secretly, my fault I suppose. Sarah said it was a bad thing I did trying to hitch you to Colin.'

Polly put a hand on his arm. 'Bert, you're not ever to think about it, it's all in the past and you have my eternal gratitude for taking Billy in.'

'Hmm, he's a good lad and if he wants a job at Mimosa he'd be more than welcome.' They turned into a track leading to Mimosa. 'Welcome back, Polly, I hope we can be friends in the future.'

'No question about that.'

'Mimosa isn't that far from Four Seasons, we can keep in touch, we'll be your nearest neighbour. Sarah will be delighted.'

'I'll be living in Fremantle, I've a job there, and miraculously my two brothers are there.'

'Well, that's good, but I still think you'll end up at Four Seasons. Anyone with half an eye can tell that Jack Peterson's smitten by you. He . . . '

'Oh no. No, Bert, he's already engaged, he's going to marry Helen, Ken Reynolds' daughter.'

'What? No, that can't be right, Helen Reynolds has run off with Joe Weston, I heard all about it in our local store. News like that spreads faster than a bush fire here. Everyone around here knows that was on the cards. Local sheep shearers told me way back that trouble was brewing at Ken Reynolds'.'

'But . . . how . . . are you sure, Bert?'

'Course I'm sure. It's all an act on Jack's part, silly fools, Joe Weston is a first rate fellow, Ken's a lucky man, and here we are, home sweet home, Mimosa. Just thank our lucky stars the wind blew in the right direction on this occasion.'

Polly's head was whirling as she remembered Ken's angry visit to Four Seasons, and the meeting afterwards behind closed doors in the study.

'Shall I wake Billy up?' Jack asked as they went into the house.

'No, no, course not, and Sarah will be asleep, I suppose,' Polly said.

'I should think so, after her medication, the others won't be long. I'll get Vera, Colin's fiancée, to rustle up some supper, you'll see Sarah in the morning.'

It was strange stepping back into the homestead, another era, though it wasn't that long ago that she and Billy had left. It had been a very long day and it seemed an age since she'd seen Sam and Fred, but it was only that morning. The thought whirled in her head — Jack wasn't marrying Helen Reynolds. Immediately all fatigue and stiffness vanished. She would peep in on Billy, then check Sarah.

Both Billy and Sarah were fast asleep. Polly sent up a prayer of gratitude for Billy's safety then went to meet Colin's fiancée, Vera, and gave a hand in the kitchen. It was an odd situation but she took to Vera straightaway.

Colin had proudly introduced his fiancée, a plump woman about ten years older than him. Polly noticed how clean, tidy and sparkling everything was and a hot supper was on the table ten minutes after Jack and the others arrived at Mimosa. Bert seemed in his element as he raised his glass of ale to toast the visitors and thank God for a happy outcome of what could have been a dreadful tragedy.

Much later when the house was quiet Polly crept into the room where she and

Billy had slept just to reassure herself he was still alive. The air was hot and oppressive, and far away thunder still rumbled on the horizon. So much had happened that day she'd found it impossible to sleep. Still fully clothed she silently unlocked the back door, quietened the dogs and took a small lantern from the porch and went outside to the small garden where she and Mabel used to take a tea break. The air was fresher here and a small full moon shone fitfully behind thick dark clouds. She walked towards the bench where she and Mabel used to sit and gave a scream as a shape moved towards her.

'Polly? What are you doing here?'

'Jack! Thank goodness, you scared me to death.'

'I hope not. I couldn't sleep. Sorry.'

'Nor me. Too hot in the ranch house and too much has happened today. My head's spinning.'

'Come and sit down for a while, are you warm enough?'

'Yes. Vera lent me a robe. I'm pleased

she's here and is going to marry Colin.'

'Yep, very fortunate, even Bert's a changed man. I can see him counting up the progeny already and now Sarah's a little better . . . ' he tailed off, a couple of night birds hooted, tall trees creaked and groaned in the wind, 'it's been a long day, Polly, I'm so pleased Billy's safe.' He took her hand, 'I hope you will be happy in Australia now that you have family here too . . . you can settle . . . your future . . . ' he broke off and was silent for so long Polly thought he may have dozed off.

'Jack?'

'Sorry, Polly, I was . . . well I was miles away,' he pressed her hand, 'in fact miles away is where I'm going.'

'Going? Where?' Polly's heart plummeted.

'England, to see my grandparents. I know I have been there fairly recently but . . . I have to get away for a while. All this business with Joe and Helen, it's been quite a problem. I hated the pretence.'

'But the ranch, all your plans, the joining up with Ken's property, the new motor car . . . ?'

'Well, there are things I have to do in England . . . and you will be happy in Fremantle with your . . . what's his name?'

'Who? What are you talking about?'

'The fellow from Castlebridge . . . who wrote to you.'

'Wrote to me?'

'Your boyfriend . . . who's coming over to see you.'

'Boyfriend? Oh, Johnny, Johnny Clark. Jack, he's not my boyfriend, he wrote to me to tell me he's getting married and he wants me to give him some information about schools in Australia. Both he and his wife to be are teachers, they plan to settle in Australia. Johnny was never anything more than a friend.'

'But you said . . . '

'I never actually said anything, I implied it because I thought you and Helen . . . '

As if on cue dark clouds briefly

parted and the moon shone on Polly and Jack, each coming to terms with the startling revelation that both were free to declare their love for each other.

Jack took Polly in his arms. 'So I can say it, I love you, Polly Fletcher. I've loved you from the very first time I set eyes on you looking for Billy on the train. Will you marry me, Polly?'

She returned his kiss. 'Of course I will, I love you too, Jack, always have, always will.'

Discreetly the moon slid behind a cloud only coming out some time later to light Jack and Polly's path back to Mimosa Homestead where Polly's great Australian adventure really began.

* * *

A few weeks later on a beautiful sunny late summer morning Jack and Polly were married at a small private ceremony at Four Seasons Acres. Billy proudly gave his sister away, Joe Weston was best man, his wife, Helen, Polly's attendant, Sam and Fred Fletcher, the bride's brothers, were honoured guests from Fremantle.

A much larger, grander, wedding party was already being planned for later when friends and neighbours and ranch workers would hopefully be joined by Castlebridge Fletchers.

Later that day Jack drove his bride away in his new motor car — for only a brief honeymoon as the harvest was in full swing. Once clear of Four Seasons Jack stopped the car and kissed his bride passionately.

'I wanted to do that all day, Polly. A wonderful day, I'm just sorry your family couldn't be there.'

'But Uncle Harry's promising to bring the whole lot of Fletchers on the S.S. *Orient* for the biggest party ever. How shall you like being swamped by Castlebridge Fletchers?'

'He can bring as many Fletchers as he likes. Harry Fletcher is the man responsible for bringing you into my heart and for that . . . ' he kissed her passionately. 'I am everlastingly grateful.'

'Me too,' murmured Polly as she returned his kiss.

THE END

Books by Joyce Johnson
in the Linford Romance Library:

ROUGH MAGIC
BITTER INHERITANCE
HOSTAGES OF FATE
SWEET LEGACY
DARK SECRET
THE SILKEN SNARE
CHANGING FORTUNES
JOURNEY INTO DANGER
TO WIN HER LOVE
SUMMER DREAM
LOVING PIONEERS
DANGEROUS LEGACY
HERITAGE OF LOVE
LOST HEART
FOR LOVE OF AN ISLAND
IN THE LIMELIGHT
LOVE ON THE MOOR
DANGEROUS JOURNEY
DARK SHADOWS
LOVE AND WAR
HIDDEN MEMORIES
DECEPTION
LOVE'S LOST TREASURE

SUSPICIOUS HEART
EDEN IN PARADISE
SWEET CHALLENGE
FOREVER IN MY HEART
TWISTED TAPESTRIES
ALL TO LOSE
CUCKOO IN THE NEST
ROMANTIC LEGACY
LOVE'S QUEST
THE POWER AND THE PASSION

Other titles in the
Linford Romance Library:

WAITING FOR A STAR TO FALL

Wendy Kremer

Lucy and Ethan grew up together. Lucy worshipped Ethan from afar and was disenchanted when he left for university, and didn't return. She hadn't realised that this was because of his family's hidden problems. Lucy is now the village librarian and Ethan is a well-known author. When Ethan comes back to the village and into her life again, can he shed his obsession with the past? Will they master the obstacles and find each other before it's too late?